The Tree in the Garden and Other Stories

Brooks Horsley

TRUE DIRECTIONS

AN AFFILIATE OF TARCHER BOOKS

iUniverse LLC
Bloomington

THE TREE IN THE GARDEN AND OTHER STORIES

This is a work of fiction. All of the characters, names, incidents, organizations, and dialogue in this novel are either the products of the author's imagination or are used fictitiously.

iUniverse books may be ordered through booksellers or by contacting:

iUniverse LLC
1663 Liberty Drive
Bloomington, IN 47403
www.iuniverse.com
1-800-Authors (1-800-288-4677)

ISBN: 978-1-4917-2879-6 (sc)
ISBN: 978-1-4917-2878-9 (e)

Printed in the United States of America.

iUniverse rev. date: 05/20/2014

To My Wife Linda

Contents

Foreword

These stories are like old friends and I am trying to find them a new and better home; they deserve more than dusty old manila folders.

I have always enjoyed short story writers who share the background and provenance of their tales, and I will follow in their steps; at the end of each story I tell as best I can remember how it came to the light of day.

The stories were written intermittently over about 16 years, so before sending them out to seek their fortune I had them tuned up by two wonderful editors: Bill Klompus and Sarah Fisher.

This is a second tour of duty for Dr. William Klompus; he served as the model of the visionary thinker in the mid twenty first century in my book <u>And the Morning and the Evening were the First Day</u>. Bill thinks I am a closet philistine and he flagged a number of words and phrases that gave the game away. I acted on almost all his suggestions and I take full responsibility for any residual philistinism.

Sarah is a busy third year medical student who really didn't have spare time for 'uncle' Brooks' literary projects; yet she made time. She entered deeply into the spirit behind the stories and from this vantage point asked for additional paragraphs that allowed the stories to be more fully themselves.

My handwriting, always bad, has only gotten worse with the passing years. Pinkie (Tracie Thornberry) and the Orange Blossom (Karen Orange) did yeoman service in converting chicken scratch to the typed word. Pinkie, in addition to her usual brilliant work with the chicken scratch, was the model for Thulas. I had the general idea of a Thula but desperately needed details, and...there stood Pinkie: So equable her idea of a flaming temper is to gently lift her left eyebrow, intelligent, and of course, very 'pink', or feminine. She is very capable, and this is in process of robbing me of my right arm; Pinkie is middle management in a large organization and is rising fast. Indeed, so fast, she is always having to travel more and bear greater responsibilities. This, plus three kids, a husband, pets, and a mortgage - the whole ball of wax - means her days are oversubscribed; far too full for my extra typing. After typing all but the first two of these short stories, Through a Glass Darkly, The Distant Music, and The Wind and the Eagle Pinkie is retiring. It is a cruel blow and I am beginning to understand why those old testaments characters, when faced with real disasters, gravitated towards sackcloth and ashes.

A final point regarding what is an ongoing debate; Bill Klompus thought the title The Tree in the Garden so-so and suggested The Tovrah Tree, which is the Hebrew name for the tree of the knowledge of good and evil. Pinkie strongly favors The Tovrah Tree, while my wife Linda and brother Ross favor The Tree in the Garden. My authorities are divided and I chose the more conventional title less from conviction than to get the story named. If anyone has any convictions on the matter please share them. I am curious as to where the balance of opinion lies.

Gone the Rainbow

L oyal was finishing her lunch and pondering the upcoming elections in Chile when a conversation at a nearby table momentarily caught her attention. A spectacled graduate student held the floor, and in an entirely serious manner, not a hint of levity, he asked his two companions; "When did you last see a rainbow?"

"Aw, Ross, not that again! I've told you before, and apparently I must tell you again; rainbows come and go on their own schedule and rarely are sufficiently memorable to make an impression. Whether or not I remember the last rainbow has precious little connection with whether there was a rainbow anytime recently." Then, on the odd whim, the beleaguered buddy asked; "Ross, try this out; when did you last see a Carta Blanca beer? If you can't think of a recent occasion does this imply there have been no Carta Blanca beers in your neighborhood? I think not. You are strongly tuned to Guinness and other beers are categorized as "not-Guinness" and not individually noted. It is more a question of focus than whether a particular non-Guinness brand is present or absent."

The third member of the trio, an attractive and hitherto quiet blond, entered the conversation; "Will, that a question has a focus, or attention component, does not mean the question is entirely subjective. The question may be objective, but getting an adequate answer may not be straightforward or easy. It is possible rainbows are gone, and if they are, then your sophisticated cleverness will systematically blind you to the truth."

Then turning to Ross she said; "Ross, I remember a wonderful rainbow from two years ago, and for the life of me I can't recall any since. Now that you mention it this seems odd, but I can't say I find it alarming."

Ross was mollified and returned to his obsession; "Will, I like your Carta Blanca illustration. Answering the Carta Blanca query retrospectively is like so much retrospective data -- it is hard to arrive at solid conclusions because of hidden focus, or selection factors. However, the Carta Blanca and rainbow problems are very simple when studied prospectively. Suppose I started paying attention to specific beers and rainbows, and I go where they are to be found. Very soon I will discover how prevalent they are. Three months ago I started looking for rainbows. Sun after rain, sprinklers, waterfalls, you name it and I sought it. I am telling you, rainbows are gone, and the only question is why!"

Graduate students love examining the curious hypothetical, and on the assumption rainbows are gone they theorized energetically and ingeniously. A bemused Loyal found none of the theory very plausible, but the energetic free play of mind made her realize how much she enjoyed being a graduate student. She organized her food tray to leave and had half risen from her chair when a sudden premonition of utter ruin struck her; she fell back into her chair physically chilled. How?! From whence the sudden

foreboding? Then she remembered. Percolating up from childhood came the recollection; after destroying the world with the great flood God had put rainbows in the sky as a sign of his covenant with man to never destroy the world again. That was it! She, proud and clever grad student, had been struck down by fairytales from childhood. How silly! How Bizarre! Even so she rushed to put a little "science" between herself and the dark fairytale. She reviewed the speculations of her fellow students willing them to be true. She reminded herself that Latin American studies was her area and conclusions she might reach in the physical sciences weren't likely to be reliable. Loyal was smart and independent, and in the final tally she could not be serious about the subtle industrial contaminant Will had urged; the 'contaminant' was altogether too selective and ad hoc to be credible. It absorbed light at all the wavelengths of the rainbow, yet water remained clear and transparent; she could see all the usual colors through her glass of water. The Greenies were always yelling about something, but had plankton and other aquatic plant life shut down there would be a huge impact on the food chain and she would have heard their howls and roars. Most wavelengths, as judged by plants and her eyes, were getting through water. The only time light got absorbed was when it was time for rainbows. She tried a more fundamental approach -- could water somehow not refract light? On her understanding of high school physics and Snell's law this was not possible. The foreboding returned, and when she rose from lunch the foreboding went with her and wrapped itself more tightly around her. Like a python, it slowly began to suffocate Loyal.

Fortunately, it was Thursday and Loyal was planning on going home to Louisville for the weekend. Her mother was a professor of Geriatrics at the University Med Center and her dad had a large practice in plastic surgery with sub-specialization in hand. Both were educated sensible people whose judgment she valued highly. Yet her parents were very different, and between them offered a rich variety of good and interesting opinion. Her mom lived in a pretty standard scientific universe and had the usual prejudices of the age in which she lived; yet her interpretations of things was clever and interesting. Her dad lived in a larger more open universe than her mom and Loyal never quite knew what he might say. In this particular case it was her dad who she suspected might help her.

Late Friday afternoon Loyal left Vanderbilt and drove up 65 N to the St. Matthews suburb of Louisville. That afternoon her dad had left for a hand meeting in Dallas and wasn't due back till Sunday afternoon. This was a setback, but Loyal was philosophic and decided she wouldn't leave Sunday afternoon till she talked with him. Loyal and her mom made a great dinner and planned Saturday. Before leaving Vanderbilt Loyal had already settled how they were going to spend Saturday; they would do their favorite hike at the Cumberland Falls State Resort Park, then linger around the Cumberland Falls and view it from every angle. In her experience, based on four or five visits, there were always rainbows available, and usually pretty good ones! The weather forecast was outstanding, with emphasis on sunny.

Her mom was both a strong and keen walker and was sincerely charmed with Loyal's plan. They got up early and were on the Cumberland River Trail by 10 a.m. Several hours later they crested the Pinnacle Knob fire tower, and from its top the world never looked so beautiful and secure. Yet as she descended the steps of the fire tower the python flexed its steely coils -- soon all gone, gone like ashes in the wind! By the bottom Loyal was in a cold sweat.

Twenty minutes later they joined the Moonbow Trail and the rugged beauty filled every sense. By the time they arrived at the Cumberland Falls Loyal's good mood was restored. She then recruited her mom to aid in her search, and they sought rainbows above the falls, below the falls, and from every angle. They returned to their car, crossed the river, and viewed the falls from the Eagle Falls Trail. There was not a hint of a rainbow. They asked two different rangers, and neither had seen a rainbow in months and months. Chilling tendrils of conviction were in place and growing.

As they drove home Loyal told her story to her mom. Her mom listened attentively and without comment until she finished. Then; "Loyal, you've got the wrong parent. This tale is for your dad; he'll have some curious little cubbyhole for your rainbows."

Loyal smiled; "Right you are, and he'll get his chance tomorrow afternoon. And yourself? Any thoughts?"

Her mom hesitated; "What I have to say is pretty tame and not likely to satisfy. Don't be a victim of words, they are very abstract and leave out much. For example, consider this; "Rainbows are produced by light being refracted by aerolized water". Yet, the sun comes out after one rain and nothing happens, then it shines after a second rain and there is a beautiful bow. In both cases we have sunshine and aerolized water. The abstractions hide a lot of subtle conditions that are critical. Suppose storms, when divided into appropriate categories, have six or seven types. Types 1-3 typically produce rainbows, types 4-7 usually don't. Suppose global warming, El Nino, or God knows what, is shifting us towards categories 4-7. If rainbows really are disappearing then this would be the direction I'd look. In any event, I suspect the world is going to limp on pretty much as usual."

Loyal thanked her mother and changed the topic. Her mother had been right; Loyal didn't find this helpful. Especially as they'd spent a sunny day with nothing but good weather by a waterfall that in the past had never failed to produce rainbows under these very conditions. Loyal failed to see what categories 1-7 rainstorms had to contribute.

They stopped in Lexington at the Joseph Beths Bookstore and both were fortunate enough to browse their way to unexpected and interesting books. After shopping they dined at an expensive and excellent restaurant that was up to the professor's standards and well beyond Loyal's. When they finally made it home mother and daughter collapsed right into their beds and slept like babies.

As occasionally happens Loyal went to bed with deep rooted worries and woke up refreshed and with a plan; sleep had indeed knit up the raveled sleeve of care. After coffee Loyal posted several notices on the various internet bulletin boards favored by the scientific community at Vanderbilt. She then phoned Tom Gulley, a senior grad student in astronomy and a buddy of hers.

"Good morning, Tom. Hope I didn't wake you."

"You didn't, but it was a near thing; what's up?"

"What do you make of this Kali thing, Tom?"

"What Kali thing? You pulling my leg? Who is Kali?"

"Kali is the consort of Lord Shiva, and a very dark goddess. Apparently every 5,000 years she destroys the world, and it is coming up soon."

"I'm sorry she's got her panties in a wad, Loyal, but what has this to do with me so early on Sunday morning?"

"The report, the legend, is that the destruction comes from the sky. This would suggest an asteroid, which is the particular province of astronomy graduate students. Before this hits the National Enquirer and talk shows perhaps you and others could make a quick scan of the heavens and announce that all is well, that Kali was kidding."

"Loyal, the astronomy community is constantly looking for asteroids and I haven't heard a thing."

"I know, Tom, but perhaps you and colleagues might review the data with a greater degree of suspicion. Assume there is an asteroid and make a best guess where it might be then follow these possibilities for a week."

"You worried Loyal?"

"Not much, but some - don't forget the dinosaurs. Review the various internet bulletin boards and see what you think. When you announce all is well let it be accurate and authoritative, not merely mindless officialiese."

"Let me look over what's out there and I'll get back to you. I may need to take you out to dinner some evening so as to explore the Kali business more thoroughly."

"Tom, if you settle this business in a workman-like way we'll have a celebratory dinner as my treat; perhaps one of those ultra fine South Pacific fusion restaurants you go on about."

You're on, money bags; start saving."

▧ ▧ ▧

At 3:15 her dad arrived. Loyal got him to a drink and a comfortable chair, then told her story. When finished, she asked her dad for his opinion.

"It sounds reasonable; in fact, it's the way I'd probably do it."

This was vintage Dad, and consequently a bit exasperating; "Revered elder, what do you mean, 'This is the way I'd do it'?"

Her dad smiled at her, "I mean if I were God I'd probably rig the rainbow business the way he seems to have."

"Exactly how did 'He' rig it?!", asked Loyal, with conspicuous patience.

"God built the all's well sign into natural processes; and, I might add, a very beautiful sign it is. The highly significant thing, the supernatural thing, is the absence of the expected, natural sign. As I recall this indicates major difficulties up ahead. In fact, the consequences are so ghastly that even the small chance they might be coming needs serious attention. Looking down the road comes first, fine points of interpretation comes a distant second. Any steps taken towards looking for upcoming disasters?", asked her dad.

"I spent the morning on the worst and most easily detected disasters. If these are not on the radar screen, I'll pick your brain for subtle ones."

"Please don't overlook my recurring nightmare", said her dad.

Loyal laughed; "You old phony!, you don't have any recurring nightmares. I never met anyone who sleeps so well as yourself."

"Well if I were going to have one it would be a large, fast asteroid with a very low albedo coming at us out of the sun. Loyal, when you notify your astronomy chums please have them pay close attention to immediately before dawn and just after or near sunset. And get radar studies on the sunny side of dear old Earth, which, by the by, seems dearer by the moment."

"All taken care of, Dad, said a distinctly smug Loyal and now clarify a final point. You have very quickly come up with what I consider the right answers, and this strengthens and gratifies me. The rainbows really should be there, and their absence lies outside the natural order. Thousands of years ago a connection between rainbows and natural disasters is recorded. Since we don't know what is going on and the stakes are so very high we need to at least spend a little time on the natural disaster angle."

"Exactly my take", said her dad, "and I sincerely hope we don't find anything."

"So," Loyal continued, "the last puzzle is this; we have a man who never goes to church, never prays, tries to keep the supernatural out of things, and never talks about God. What does this man do when faced with the rainbow puzzle? He is immediately cheek and jowl with the deity comparing notes as to how he would have done it. I'm not against or for this Bill and Ed sort of thing, I'm only trying to understand where it comes from."

Her dad smiled; "Boo, you don't think an angry asteroid zipping towards you is a good reason to brush away cobwebs and mend fences? This isn't the time for a little cozy cozy?"

Boo had to laugh; "I suppose it is, but I asked the question seriously and what I'm hearing, while not a bifurcated tongue, is tongue in cheek."

"Actually it is very simple and very reasonable. I live in beautiful mountain country, and, for that matter, so does everyone else. I like mountain country, and as I walk along, my focus is on the meadow before me, the stream burbling along beside me, and the immediate stony eminence. What does not catch my attention is elaborate explanations for why the country 'really' is or isn't one elaborate mountain, or why this one mountain is or isn't a talking mountain. Mountain country is good enough for me."

"Dad, this is good as far as it goes, but doesn't cover the Bill and Ed episode."

"Now remember", went on her dad, "As I walk along I'm open minded about talking mountains; I'm neither favorable nor opposed. Then one day a mountain speaks to me in perfectly good English. What should I do? Pretend it is the burbling stream? Grunt? Hum a song? Surely the appropriate response is to speak politely in English to the mountain."

"Come on, Dad", said an exasperated Loyal, "I summarized our position in a way you found entirely adequate and never mentioned God or talking mountains."

"Your summary was entirely adequate for immediate practical purposes, and had no need to disturb what is implicit in the rainbow affair. The natural order is altered in a very selective and specific way, and there is absolutely no logical connection between this alteration and natural disasters. The connection is by agreement and convention; it is a sign. You can dance all around it in very clever ways, but when the smoke clears you are left with a sign. Signs assume purpose and mind and are the roots of conversation. Hence, as you put it, the Bill and Ed aspect."

"Does this change things between you and The Mountain?", asked Loyal.

"Less than you think. It seems to me that many people who believe they are conversing with the mountain and really conversing with themselves. If my impression is wrong then the mountain sure tells people a lot of crazy and contrary things. For my part I like the mountainous aspect of mountains and am less charmed with the conversational aspects. If the mountain wants to talk it knows where I am; in the meantime, when it comes to conversation, I prefer my fellow man."

Later, after an early supper and before Loyal started the drive back to Nashville, her mom took her aside; "Sweetheart, I overhead some of what your father said. The wretched man may not be good for much, but he has an excellent nose for the margins of science. I have no conviction in the matter, but I am getting concerned. Please let me know the moment you find anything. As it is I think I'll go ahead and get refundable tickets to New Zealand for two months from now. Also, I'll make initial steps to get medical licenses in New Zealand."

Loyal was surprised; "Mom, for a woman with no conviction that's pretty aggressive behavior!"

"Not really. It costs very little time and effort and could mean everything if your fears are realized. Should a large asteroid hit on our side of the northern hemisphere I want to be on the opposite side of the globe in an English speaking country with a strong government of law."

"Isn't the 'English speaking' portion of that thought a bit parochial? Mom, you've always been a liberal's liberal; what has come over you?"

"I'm still a liberal's liberal, but suppose conditions in our country should become desperately hard and there is limited room at the trough. Who is likely to get priority; a fellow Christian speaking English, or a little yellow man spouting gibberish? Under desperate circumstances I don't want to stress anyone's prejudices. And should the disaster be plague, then an isolated, homogeneous island like New Zealand is your best chance. Should an asteroid land far from us then we'll stay put. I just want a choice."

Loyal was surprised and intrigued at her mom's response to possible disaster, so she pursued it a bit; "Mom, what happens if there is an asteroid heading our way, we move to New Zealand, and then the asteroid misses or is deflected?

"That would be wonderful news for Mother Earth and our species. If you manage to give me even one day of advanced warning then we will all be able to retire."

"How so?", asked the otherworldly grad student.

"If I get the news before the rest of the world I'll sell all our stocks and put the money in gold. The news comes, the market crashes. The disaster passes and we buy back in at the bottom of the market."

Loyal was thoroughly impressed; with her mom around, a mom amongst moms, who needed a guardian angel!

"Any other preparations?" she asked.

Her mom smiled; "Just the obvious ones. If you give me a bit of advanced notice, I'll be able to stock our summer cabin with tons of rice, beans, lentils, and dried meat. Within a day or two of the news the supermarkets will be empty -- nothing left to buy. So it really matters; please get me early news, even hours will help."

That evening, as Loyal drove south on 65, she considered how blessed she was in her parents. She had arrived Friday evening with crushing doubt and fear. Now, Sunday evening, she drove back to Vanderbilt supported in thought and deed, at peace, and even in a subdued sort of way, happy.

Thursday afternoon at 2:30 p.m. Loyal phoned her mom; "Mom, Kali has a 60 km diameter and is due to touch down in about six weeks, probably somewhere in the south pacific. For Dad's information, it is coming out of the sun and was detected by radar. The news will be released 10 a.m. eastern time tomorrow, so you'd better get busy doing whatever you plan to do. At the risk of spoiling you I plan to come home again this weekend. I love you. Give Dad a hug for me. Bye."

Saturday evening was cold and rainy, but inside "the cabin" all was cheery and snug. Loyal and her parents sat around a warm and friendly fire. They hadn't put away all the dried food yet and the floor was still covered. The professor had gotten them out of the stock market and into gold. The supermarket cupboards were bare.

"Boo, I'm proud of you!", said her dad; "Your use of the internet to recruit the amateur and professional astronomers to your cause was brilliant."

Loyal smiled contentedly; "You give me too much credit. Friends of mine in astronomy did most of the work."

"Did you dream up the 'vedic millennium' and Kali's return?", asked her mother.

"I plead guilty. I also concocted the two respectable and independent psychics. The spirit animating the astronomers was; 'This is bullshit, but it is scary bullshit. Let's clear it off the board right now!"

"Now it is your turn, Dad. I read the account of the flood in Genesis, and it is quite clear; a vindictive God destroyed the world because of its sinfulness. He then promised not to do it again, but now he has backtracked on his promise, removed the sign of his pledge, and is winding up for another try. Your mountain chum ain't no sweety. I understand your reticence about conversing with him."

"That's how the story goes", agreed her dad, "but it is not the way I see it. Last week I mentioned that many conversations with the mountain are really people conversing with themselves. More often it isn't so simple, rather it is a bit of mountain and a bit of self. The story told is that of a self-righteous old gentleman conveying a bit of mountain and a bit of self. I see a wonderful early warning system. In any event, as I understand it, we have an excellent chance of breaking up the asteroid with deep penetration thermonuclear warheads. We are going to run through some major debris and will unavoidably have many significant problems, but it probably won't be the knockout blow it might have been had it not been for a fine graduate student of my acquaintance. And if the damn thing does get through there's your mom; she's tough and doesn't sink easily."

Then, as an afterthought; "Boo, you may be in a position to judge for yourself. Suppose we weather the storm, and a few months later the rainbow comes back. Wouldn't that suggest a wonderful providence providing early warning of impending apocalypses? The mountain trying hard to save your stiff neck and uncircumcised heart, not break it"

Gone the Rainbow

This story has its roots in a weekend outing to Cumberland Falls State Resort Park. The day was lovely and there were beautiful rainbows at the Cumberland Falls. In an idle moment I subtracted the rainbows and started playing with the implications. The drive home was several hours, and near journeys end the story was more or less finished, except for the writing, which was several months later.

The Devil's Shiny Lure, Or
A Young Terrorist Dreams
The Impossible Dream

John Ransom grew to strong manhood at a time his country suffered deeply and day by day grew more a stranger to hope. The author of these sorrows was a hard and exacting tyrant who steadily dispensed injustice and cruelty to a people who had long enjoyed a happy tradition of freedom.

It was John Ransom's study by day and by night to free his country. But turn where he might the tyrant's strength loomed over him like a vast mountain. To crush the tyrant seemed impossible, yet such was John's nature that to not crush the tyrant revolted his very soul. He writhed in the grip of his dilemma until at last, with many misgivings, he reluctantly journeyed to the castle of the Dark Lord.

The Dark Lord had been awaiting John's visit and he listened carefully and politely to the details of John's situation. At length, John finished and asked for aid. The Dark Lord considered the matter gravely and carefully.

Then the Dark Lord spoke, in a voice low and like the winter twig that scrapes the pane on the frosty night; "It is a strong and dangerous current you would enter. If the roots of your resolve do not reach far and run deep many will be swept to ruin. Your resolve must be strong indeed, for early in the struggle my creatures will be but poorly formed and must feed directly on your will and resolve. This condition is but brief, and soon they will stand alone, but even then they must be fed and tended with care. If I give you aid will you guard my creatures like a father?"

John looked beyond the Dark Lord and beheld his creatures; a more fell and malignant brood he had never seen. His heart fell, but he made a final venture; "Are there no others?"

"I have what I have. If these please you not then seek elsewhere."

It was a bitter pill, but John swallowed it; "I accept your creatures. Are there no other conditions?"

"None. Only tend my creatures with care. It is in the nature of things that I will reap more than I sow."

John yet again knew deep doubt, and said; "I feared as much. Even so I will take your creatures."

And John Ransom took the Dark Lord's creatures and departed.

The war that now enveloped the land was hard and pitiless, and no quarter was asked or given. In the press of events, and much to his dismay, John found that he had to clutch the Dark Lord's creatures to his bosom or perish. They grew from things hesitant and tremulous to become creatures of fierce and terrible power. Indeed, their power was irresistible, and as the eighth year of war drew to a close the tyrant and his power were utterly destroyed.

The fall of the tyrant occasioned general rejoicing, but in the subsequent months of peace dark rumors began to circulate, and ere long the truth was clear to all. The Dark Lord's creatures were entrenched throughout the land and their meat was human flesh and their drink was human misery.

John Ransom did not waste a moment on self-pity or false hopes but rather traveled hard for the Dark Lord's castle. He entered the Dark Lord's presence with a concealed dirk and the resolve that he would not leave the room without removing the Dark Lord's creatures from the land. However, he did not proceed at once to desperate and extreme measures, but rather showed the equanimity in the midst of danger and decision for which he was justly famous.

The Dark Lord asked his business and he replied with calm good cheer; "My Lord, I suspect you know my problem, but the fact is that I must remove your creatures from my country and I would appreciate your advice on the matter."

The Dark Lord smiled a mirthless smile; "Ah, truly that is the question. You must lead them to greener pastures, and these pastures must be in someone else's country. For example, Pope Clement sent my creatures of an earlier age on crusades against the infidel."

John answered quietly, but with finality; "I will never lead your creatures into another man's country. Tell me of other ways."

The Dark Lord smiled yet again; "It is a moral education to hear you speak. You will never lead my creatures into the other man's country, but you lead them willingly enough into your own country."

John remained equable; "Times change. What I once did I will not do now. Bearing this in mind talk to the man you see before you. Tell me another way."

The Dark Lord sighed and spoke; "I am disappointed in you, John. It is possible you do not see how things are?"

John remained business-like and cheerful; "I see what I see. Tell me, my Lord, what do you see?"

"Those creatures you call mine are now more truly yours. You have played the father so long and so well that it has become truth. And you John, have become a part of me; you are now my creature. By my art you may see this directly. Look me in the eye and know the truth."

John looked full in the Dark Lord's face, and knew he spoke truth. Even so John remained cheerful and confident in manner and it irked the Great Lord and worried him, though he was at pains to hide it.

At length, John spoke; "There is much truth in what you say, but it is not the whole and complete truth. The portion of me that lies beyond your reach is critical and includes the core of my will. For example, I can tell you to kiss my ass and really mean it. Were I entirely your creature how could this be?"

"A wise man in olden days once said that if thine eye offend thee then pluck it out. This saying strikes me as solid good sense. If I am part of you then you are a part of me. Take advantage of the knowledge this makes possible; look in my eye and know beyond certainty that you must take your portion of me and depart. There is no middle ground."

And the Dark Lord stooped down and looked closely in John Ransom's eye and saw that it was so.

Many years later on a rainy autumn evening a beautiful young woman chatted gaily with her beau on the edge of the Great Autumn Ball. The door opened and a tall, somewhat gaunt gentleman of advancing middle years entered. As he handed his rain drenched cloak to an attendant he turned and the young woman saw that a patch covered his right eye and his right arm was gone.

Involuntarily she grabbed her beau's arm saying; "Charles, something terrible must have happened to the poor man!"

Charles followed her gaze and went white as a sheet. Ignoring his lady friend he stammered; "A thousand pardons Lord Ransom."

John cast a serene and happy glance at the couple; "No pardon required. You friend's kind heart becomes her like a crown."

Then turning to the beautiful young woman he said; "My lady, these wounds are dear to me, and I would neither trade them nor forget them."

Then turning he walked into the happy gathering his wounds made possible.

And John's countrymen called him blessed and he came to be known as the father of his country.

Dream

I took this story from my eleven year old son Ross; I wonder if he remembers? The son has a strong and original turn of mind which, despite stern efforts to smother the poor thing every now and then <u>will</u> break out. I used to make up stories for the kids and one afternoon, against this background, we were discussing stories and sharing particularly vivid, good stories. At length I asked him if he had any new stories. As it happened he did. He had recently seen a movie with monsters in it and had been vaguely disappointed, yet at the same time intrigued. The upshot was his own story, which grew out of the movie but with significant changes. A land is troubled with terrible monsters. In desperation this peril is countered with a smaller, 'good' monster. The 'good' monster clears out the bad monster. Unfortunately the good monster has a tricky life cycle that had not been understood and ultimately winds up embedded in the host country as an ineradicable evil far worse than the original monster. What you don't know can kill you! For some reason, Ross' monster vividly evoked terrorism: well intended even high minded men use a terrible tool, briefly as they see it, for the highest ends. Unfortunately they are molded by their 'tools' and the story ends badly.

So far everything is simple and clear, and I wrote the story within a few days of Ross telling his story. Now, looking back many years later the curious thing is <u>how</u> I told the story. This story could be told many ways and the epic bard-like tone is not the most obvious. There were many choices, but at the time I was never aware of the choice, there was only the way I went; it was the immediate clear way.

The Walk

—◄ ▣ ►—

There! It had done it again! A drop of water hanging from the leaf, (wasn't it called dew?), had caught the starshine just so, and had been transformed to a brilliant incandescence. He shifted his position slightly in an effort to recover the magic, but the thing was elusive and eventually he returned his attention to the small game trail he hoped would lead him to the mountains crest.

The trail meandered through mossy glens and past and across small merry little streams, but seemed unable to commit to ascending the mountain. At last, with some reluctance, he left his pleasant companion of the past half hour and headed directly up the mountain. The grade was, as of yet, gentle. The trees were towering giants with the attendant blessings of an open forest floor and, later in the morning, shade. The air was still and fresh.

▣ ▣ ▣

It was an old, old system. The aging G-type star was now a venerable red giant bordering the original home planet.

Remarkably man was still in this system and possessed a pedigree extending back into the mists of millions of years. To all appearances man had changed very little. Even more remarkably man had not destroyed himself in internecine war, had not perished in any natural or microbial apocalypse, and had never damaged his original home planet past repair. Perhaps responsible stewardship would be pitching it rather high, but man <u>had</u> been both lucky and ingenious.

As their star moved closer man eventually had to stop the rotation of the home planet. Man lived on the shady side of the planet and farmed the margins. There were vast underground cities. This worked well for a long, long time, but eventually man developed and modified a planet with a larger and more distant orbit, a Mars-like planet.

Gradually, over eons man shifted to the new planet and the original home was abandoned. The forests, mountains, seas, flowers of the original home became a misty half dream. Then, except for a few scholars, it was gone.

Man endured and the star grew. Eventually the rotation of the Mars-like planet was stopped and satellites of the yet more distant gas giants were developed. It was in these times our story begins.

▦ ▦ ▦

The shifting pattern of shade created by the breeze and the dancing leaves was a subtle thing that fascinated the walker.

While resting on the margin of a hillside meadow he carefully watched the way the shade played over his legs and abdomen. At length he once more shouldered his pack and resumed his journey. At another meadow with a small lake he came across dragonfly like insects and greatly enjoyed the way the starshine played on their wings and the water.

As he was leaving this meadow he came face to face with a large mammal. This animal had big soft eyes and seemed to have no harm in it. Years ago, while scanning several extremely ancient texts he vaguely remembered mention of 'deer' and it sounded similar to this animal; he felt a thrill of kinship. The walker also must have seemed benign and the two mammals spent a thoughtful social moment. At length the animal moved past him and towards the water. The animal had never seen a man before and had been curious.

By now the walker was high enough that things had cooled to the point where the warm starshine felt wonderful on his back; he savored it. Again, from ancient volumes he remembered mention of this 'sun on one's back' and felt kinship and solidarity of the long lost home planet.

■   ■   ■

It was in the air, and at the back of everyone's mind; a star mission to plant man in a new and younger system. This was a late moment in our story, and though such moments might come again, yet it was sufficiently late this was no longer certain. When this system had died and the story ended there would have been a last star mission; perhaps this was it. There were records of long past missions, but not many. Strangely there was no longer any contact with these missions. After a few hundred years interest would flag and the conversations had always drifted into silence. An elaborate radar setup was in place to detect messages from beyond our system, but none ever came.

A beautiful, large starship was designed and built. It had room for thirty thousand souls, and included parks, restaurants, malls and other ingredients vital to human wellbeing and happiness. Things necessary to life were ingeniously recycled and preserved. The ship was a wonder and a marvel that stretched our resolve and ingenuity. Vital and limited resources were used with a prodigality that would have dismayed all but the most hopeful, but hope burned brightly in every breast. The thirty thousand expedition members were carefully selected for skills and social qualities; the number that would gladly have gone greatly exceeded the number of positions available.

At length the colonists and their ship departed, traveling towards the nearest likely star. Earlier mistakes were to be strictly avoided and there was extensive and ritualized communication with the aging mother system.

The ship traveled for several generations before arriving at the nearest likely star. All went well and the colonists arrived in good health and spirits.

■   ■   ■

As the walker moved higher the trees thinned and he came to know the wonders of wind, starshine, and view. The day was most fair, the breezes positively caressing, and viewing from the heights bred high and pleasant thoughts. The walker thought of his wife and children, and wished they could share the high places with him.

He found a cluster of shrublike plants that had many small berries on them. He tried the berries and discovered they were delicious. He spent awhile picking and eating the berries (blueberries?) and then sat down to digest them and enjoy the view. The warm starshine felt even better than before and he dozed off. When he awoke he noticed a bird soaring far above him, vivid against the deep blue sky (hawk? eagle?). There was something wonderfully lonely and poignant about that soaring bird. Had men on the distant home planet seen and felt it too?

▦   ▦   ▦

The new star had <u>the</u> perfect planet! Exactly the same size and orbit as their original home planet! It was vacant; it was theirs! It was Eden!! Even so, they were careful. Robotic craft cruised, filmed and sampled the planet. Pets were placed on the planet and returned with smiles and tans.

The final test was for a group of ten people to live on the planet surface for a few months.

In view of the smiling and tanned pets and other tests this seemed cautious past reason, but Tom Neely, the chief planetologist in charge of early settlement, would not yield.

A shuttle loaded with the pioneers and their equipment was duly dispatched. They landed in a beautiful meadow. The shuttle stayed with them for twenty-four standard hours and during this time all things entering the shuttle were carefully sterilized and exposed to prolonged vacuum conditions. The shuttle pilot, Marge Stillman, was great friends with Beth Tate, one of the pioneers. Just before the shuttle returned to the ship, in the twenty-fifth hour, so to speak, Beth stood under the nose of the craft waving frantically. She had found what appeared to be a pinecone and wanted Marge to have it for her daughter's upcoming tenth birthday. Both Marge and Beth felt Tom Neely was the last word in all matters pertaining to old ladies and stupid protocol. Both women raced to the airlock, waived protocol, and passed the pinecone in. What a delightful gift!

Forty-eight hours later everyone in the pioneer group was dead and the plague was beginning on the ship. The deadly agent was a virus that caused extensive demyelination of the central nervous system and an utterly destructive vasculitis. The agent was very hardy, and very, very infectious. There was no treatment, and no time to develop one. People died, and died, and died.

◼ ◼ ◼

At length the walker's attention left the soaring bird and returned to his journey. He ate a last few berries and had a drink. Then struggled to his feet and continued up the mountain. The way was steeper and rougher than earlier and there were many stones.

The stones and roughness gave rise to an unusual line of thought. Of late the walker's customary travel paths were soft, uniform, and lonely; at times he had felt ghostly and unreal to himself. By contrast he could now feel the hard stones under his feet, the breeze on his face, the starshine on his back; he felt alive, and real, and if he didn't mind his step he could turn his ankle. It was all so vibrant…so planetary.

◼ ◼ ◼

Desperate and draconian measures were taken, and seemed to work, for awhile; but these periods of relative quiet always proved evanescent, and the dying went on and on. To Tom Neely and his friend Mike Fisher, an immunologist, the nightmare made no sense. How could this virus so perfectly target specifically human receptors? Life on the planet was varied and abundant, and their cats and dogs suffered no harm. Tom studied the planet very closely with new eyes, looking for human artifacts. There were none.

So he looked again, easing up on his notion of an artifact. Also he began looking over the planets natural satellites, or moons; there were two. Gradually his attention came to rest on a hill in the southern hemisphere that seemed a little too hemispherical. Also, on the larger moon there was an area too smooth and free of craters. Tom and a few other scientifically inclined survivors took the shuttle to the hemisphere. In space garb they drilled into its core. This was purely in an effort to understand, since the expedition had long since passed the point of no return. Also, it helped fill an aching void; Tom's wife and two children had attended Kaitlan Stillman's party and had handled the wonderful pinecone.

◙　◙　◙

Since the misty, early days of Old Earth the man climbing a mountain has had his heart broken by mountain shoulders. There stands the 'crest', and it's not that far. The walker climbs with renewed hope and strains every sinew, after all, he's almost there! But, alas, his 'crest' proves to be yet another shoulder.

Our walker recapitulated this ancient theme twice. At the same time he was becoming acquainted with another ancient truth. Physical training is a wonderful thing, and our walker had exercised much of late, but the virtue imparted is more context specific than we reckon. A man who trains his legs on bicycles no doubts helps his walking too, but not nearly so much as might be expected.

Our walker gradually realized he was not so stout a fellow as he'd imagined, and his fatigue was coming to dominate and control his thoughts. On this particular walk that would never do; he slowed markedly, and his fatigue gradually receded into the background. Secondly, he realized he would not be reaching the crest; he was way out in his calculations. It really didn't matter, and he made brief note of the fact and let it go.

The walker had gained a very considerable height and the view had come to dominate the other trail charms and points of interest. He was on a long sloping shoulder and below him was a large lake in a rugged and beautiful valley. The river supplying the lake featured much white water and several impressive waterfalls. The walker studied the scene with pleasure and appreciation. Then slowly wended his way up the trail. The quality of the late afternoon light was different than earlier, and he noted with interest the soft golden quality and the way margins were blurred and softened. He liked late afternoon light, it possessed a soft magic and was oddly calming and peaceful.

Now that the walker could cast his mind beyond the pain in his legs and his labored breathing he began reflecting on what he would not be seeing. He would not be seeing the colors of autumn. From several ancient films he'd thought fall colors wonderful. He tried to imagine them by the golden late afternoon light, and failed. Spring colors would remain on his 'to see' list. No thunderstorms. No northern dawn, or, as one ancient book had it, 'northern lights'.

The walker shrugged philosophically; unquestionably he would miss much, but there was nothing for it. On the other hand, he, a planetologist, had at last been on a planet, and had enjoyed a wonderful late summer walk in the mountains.

■   ■   ■

Tom and friends did not have an easy time getting into the hemispherical hill. It _was_ artifact, and not very far below the soil and trees they encountered a surface of diamond-like hardness; it was a synthetic material they had never before encountered. At length, after destroying several of their best drills, they entered the structure, which seemed to be fifty thousand plus years old. It was a mausoleum to man and the planet, and a warning. Etched on a large wall was a pictorial primer on the language. Whatever material was used for the etching was preternaturally durable and once the dust was removed the pictures and script were sharp and clear. Tom's computer rapidly learned the language.

Man had settled Theta one hundred thousand years ago. Five thousand years after arriving man had destroyed himself in a war where incredible technique and ingenuity had been expended on viral and bacterial agents. These agents escaped their creators control and became embedded in Theta itself. Theta became lethal to man, and man died out. The mausoleum was filled with the record of man on Theta, his history, scientific and technical achievements, works of art and music. Now man was once again on Theta and there would still be no recognition and appreciation of the works of man on Theta; the only legacy would be death and extinction. What irony! Man's legacy forever and always destroyed what it sought to inform and enrich. It was simultaneously wonderfully rich and utterly barren.

Over the next month Tom and friends discovered satellites originally designed to warn man away from Theta; all systems had failed. The warning system had long since either became orbiting debris, escaped Theta's orbit altogether, or a decaying orbit had destroyed the satellite in Theta's atmosphere. The larger moon, as Tom had suspected, proved to have wonderful artifacts and records. The moons warning system had also failed.

Over the ensuing months Tom and others ferried the pets of thirty thousand people to Theta's surface. It was a large undertaking, and a sad one. They did what they could to ease things for the animals, but ultimately the pets would have to make their own way.

During this last effort, one by one the remaining humans died; as things turned out Tom Neely was the last human in the Theta system.

In these closing days there had been an intense and urgent discussion of what to do; how to avoid future disasters. How many earlier expeditions had come to Theta? Had any survived and moved on to different systems? Had man miraculously survived in his home system only to booby trap the obvious door to the greater galaxy? Perhaps they were the exception; afterall, had Marge and Beth not breached protocol they would have been en route to a new home. But in his heart of hearts Tom could not blame them; who could have guessed?! And with thirty thousand plus humans there would always be breeches and deviations from policy.

Had man on Theta, in an effort to save our species, launched a last mission to the stars? They were very advanced, it was easily within their capabilities. Perhaps even now there were thriving human worlds in other systems. However, the records had not made mention of such a mission, and surely it would have been worth mentioning. Wishful thinking.

They thought of sending the ship back home on automatic. They could open the ship to space and this should exterminate all residual disease. Unfortunately this was not entirely certain. If the diseases should arrive in the aging mother system it could be the end of our species. The gift from the stars would be death.

Suppose they sent the ship home and it arrived without residual disease. Did that solve future problems? No, sadly it didn't. Given the time scale and the mutability of man's political arrangements and record keeping, a hundred thousand years from now it could all happen again.

They decided against sending the ship home, but they broadcasted the story to the mother system and set the system to broadcast until it failed. The ship was placed in as stable an orbit as could be managed, with possible error being towards an escape trajectory.

▦　▦　▦

The late afternoon light began to fade and insensibly progressed to a fine starset. The walker looked about for a vantage point and a comfortable seat. He found a good spot with an excellent view of the lake and supplying river. The fading light reflected off the water and he was entranced. As the epiphany faded he felt the first touch of nausea; this was expected and right on schedule. He had twenty standard minutes and he set his wrist alarm accordingly.

As the first evening stars came out the walker returned to his roots; in his mind's eye he gathered his wife Kim and his children around him. He remembered the many happy times together and the amusing incidents. The alarm went off. He opened his backpack and removed the urns with the ashes of his wife and his children. He briefly considered a flask of his favorite whiskey he'd brought along for this moment, but he didn't remove it. He reached in his pocket for a small brown pill. He put the pill in his mouth and leaned back with his arms around the ashes of his family and his eyes on the evening sky. The stars twinkled, just like the text books said. It had been a wonderful day, and Tom Neely gave a contented sigh and bit down hard on the little brown pill. The taste was most bitter, which, with a wry smile, Tom thought most appropriate. So it ended.

Walk

This is one bleak story! Mankind destroying itself on some planet is bad enough, but to do this in such a way as to generate repeat episodes which effectively block us from the stars and doom the species, well, this is a new order of bleakness.

A dark vision, even a really bleak one, is not a story, and the kernel of my story comes from a novel of monumental bleakness: Nevil Shute's <u>On the Beach</u>. In the wake of a no-holds-barred nuclear war the prevailing winds are bringing the radiation south to extinguish the remnant of mankind in southern Australia. A U.S. nuclear submarine has been in Australia for several months - there is no other port or base. The captain makes one last patrol of the west coast of North America. At night, off the coast near Seattle, a sailor takes a small boat to shore and in the morning is seen fishing off an old pier; this pier is near his home and he fished here as a boy. He is at peace, is happy, and tells the submarine to continue its patrol; this is where he wishes to make an end, not a month later in Australia amongst strangers. Everyone has been issued a cyanide pill and when nausea and misery come he has an escape. In my story the planetologist who has never seen or walked a planet wishes to make an end seeing and walking a planet.

The Tree in the Garden

The Wager

The house seemed so quiet when Kim and the kids were away. 'I suppose I should get something done,' thought Ed, but nothing cornered or pressed, and for the hundredth time his thoughts drifted back to late Saturday afternoon two weeks ago. They had been twenty miles out of town and comfortably on their way towards the Smokey Mountains for a much anticipated summer holiday. Then the car, a thing of exemplary regularity, broke down and left them stranded by the side of the road. What a letdown; it sure knocked vacation momentum on the head. Ed had just completed the timeless gesture of looking under the hood when Dee, a university colleague and particular friend of Ed's, drove by and stopped. After a brief discussion Ed phoned the state police and a towing service, then they all packed into Dee's car. Instead of driving them home Dee drove them to his house where there was a party that evening. Dee's parties were few, but invariably good, and this particular evening was even better than usual; they all had a wonderful time, especially Kim. After the party Dee drove them home, and late Monday afternoon they were back on the road for the Smokies. On the face of it Dee's arrival looked providential, and surely it was, but Ed suspected it might be something more than your garden variety providence.

Two weeks before Dee's gala Ed and family had been invited, and Ed, knowing their vacation plans, had politely declined. Dee had urged they launch their vacation with his party and leave first thing Sunday morning. There were several objections to this suggestion, upon which Dee had philosophically shrugged his shoulders. The car failure itself was thoroughly ponderable, but there really was no reason Dee should happen by as he did; the 'breakdown' was far from Dee's beaten paths. The party itself was a little unusual in that while there were other friends in attendance the food and drink had been particularly tailored to the preferences of the Ed Taylor family. Had Ed been expected this would have made sense, after all he was Dee's particular friend and Dee was 'Uncle Dee' to the boys, but the party was catered, and Ed had declined two weeks before the event, so one might have expected more generally favored food.

But these particulars were not what made Ed thoughtful; what arrested Ed's attention was the party episode having company. Strange things clustered around Dee like ticks on a dog. Dee had won not one, but two of the smaller lotteries and this did not reflect a life-long habit of buying lottery tickets but rather buying exactly one ticket on each occasion he needed money. The first time followed a spike in interest rates and Dee decided to pay off his house. The second came about from a conjunction of needing a new car and planning an unusually expensive vacation. Thinking of Dee's exotic vacation jogged Ed's memory and fueled his puzzle over how to classify Dee.

Dee was a professor of English literature at the same small midwestern university where Ed was professor of mathematics. The vacation time Dee requested from his department chairman included several months early in the fall semester and was already spoken for; even with Dee on hand there would be something of a pinch. Dee was told to pick some other vacation time, and the further he planned ahead the better chance he'd get the requested time. Dee went right on with his travel plans and at the last minute, for reasons having nothing to do with Dee, the colleague cancelled his vacation plans and the way was open for Dee.

Ed pondered these and other incidents, and his mind was like a hungry tiger prowling outside a locked house, looking for a way in. Half formed ideas presented themselves, were judged wanting, and put aside. After ten to fifteen minutes of deep thought Ed smiled, pleased with himself; while this looked like the blindest of alleys yet there was something he could do, a halting first step. He pulled out his cell phone and dialed Dee.

"Hi Dee, it's Ed. Just checking we're on for tomorrow evening at my place. I've thought of a little wager to spice our game. This Saturday evening at 7 P.M. there is a welcoming party for the young couple joining our faculty. Unless you are very out of character you will avoid it like plague, which, considering that the young woman is joining the English Department is doubly a shame to you. In an effort to keep you on the right path, here's the wager: if I win you attend the welcoming party, while if you win you can suit yourself, which, given your curmudgeonly ways, will be to plant your fat ass in an easy chair in front of the television, or read a book."

"I accept; I love a wager. Are you and Kim going to the party?"

Ed was surprised, "Of course; I'd be in no position to lecture you if I weren't."

Dee laughed; "That's never stopped you before! As to 'curmudgeon,' a brief thought and query; I am fifty, and you are thirty-eight - when you are fifty will you be nipping off to faculty welcoming parties?! If not, and I suspect your own amply upholstered ass will be planted in front of the television, does this signify you are a curmudgeon?"

Ed laughed; "Dee, you are indulging in mere obfuscation; of course you are a curmudgeon, but you are my curmudgeon and I wouldn't have you any other way. So, tomorrow evening at 7 P.M. we'll sit down and settle your fate for Saturday evening."

High Country

There was an invigorating breeze with the slightest promise
of autumn. A few clouds scudded along, but only enough
to keep the sun comfortable and out of one's eyes. It was
wonderful to be alive, and Jay felt like breaking into song.
Then out of the corner of his right eye he sensed rather than
saw something, and grew very still and quiet; thirty feet to
his right, standing against a large rock, stood a magnificent
big horn ram. The lordly beast considered him calmly and
thoughtfully. Their gazes came together and held; he felt
the indefinable but warm bond of mammalian fellowship.
At length the spell broke and the ram moved behind the
rock and then up the hill. The alpine heights held many
wonders, but few to equal such a ram! As he continued his
way down the steep barely discernible mountain path the
breeze strengthened and set a nearby meadow of alpine
flowers to dancing; and such a dance! The ram, lordly and
magnificent though he be, gave way to the charm of the
alpine meadow.

The walker made his way past the meadow and two
lower cousin meadows before finally crossing a small stream
to stand on a final crest immediately above subalpine
country. As he stood there, lingering amongst things alpine,
he studied several fluffy clouds four hundred feet below him
as they made their stately way across the valley he would be
entering. He noticed a small shadow pass swiftly over the
largest of the clouds; he looked up, and high above he saw
a golden eagle. 'Ah, to soar like that. So far above the things
of earth!', thought Jay.

For a brief way the path was so steep his attention
was entirely on his footing, but soon the grade eased and

small birch, spruce, and pine began appearing. Jay hadn't travelled far in the subalpine before he saw blueberries, which rapidly increased in both number and quality. At length he postponed his journey in their favor. After eating his fill he once again made his way to lower country.

As he was leaving subalpine country for true forest he saw a fisher, an animal found more in books than the forest in which you happen to be walking, and he crossed a river sufficiently large and fast to pose some peril. This peril was more than compensated by a profusion of large rocks ideally suited for leaping; indeed, so much so that he lingered on the river. The valley in which the river ran narrowed quite quickly so the river became faster and wilder, at which point it fell seventy feet in a spectacular waterfall to continue its journey to the sea as a broader, more sedate and middle aged river.

Our walker left the river just above the falls and carefully made his way down a cliff-like descent to the forest floor. The forest was primarily of beech and maple with a few oaks, hickory, and pine thrown in for variety. The entire area was primordial and the trees were large with very little undergrowth. The trail was broad and well demarcated and worked its way through a maze of small rugged hillocks that were cliff-like and had large picturesque rocks at their bases; individual hills were between seventy and a hundred feet in height. there was the occasional small lake and several streams needed to be jumped.

The walker loved this trail and magical forest and slowed his pace, but four to five miles and an hour and a half later he was close to home and nearing the end. The late afternoon sunshine had a golden quality as he arrived at the narrow entrance to the valley, which was guarded by two tower-like hillocks, a huge oak, and a sugar maple whose trunk was as straight as a temple column. Two squirrels sat in the maple discussing the events of the day, and the walker nodded to them as he went by. A quarter mile later the trail bifurcated; the left wended its way to a country lane and his home, while the right led to a small park with a tree and a fountain. The park both intrigued and puzzled the walker and he visited it frequently, but it was late and he needed to get home. The walker went left and was soon on a wooded country lane. His home stood in twenty acres of beautiful lawn with stately trees and artfully placed terraces and fountains. The house itself was two hundred yards back from the road and was built of stone covered in ivy. He always loved coming home, and doubly so tonight since his wife Ann was cooking lamb and had baked one of her apple pies. He was halfway down his meandering driveway when the silver bell chimed.

The Chess Game

Ed could think of a million ways coincidence could work against a man in a given chess game: full bladder, low grade background worries, an attractive woman's bare legs, mind working part time on other problems, and the list goes on. For this particular match he made a real effort to reduce the scope of damaging coincidence; he meant to play truly high level chess. Within the university Ed was recognized as one of the best players, while few even knew Dee played chess. Dee played with Ed, and nowhere else; it was very much a talented amateur against an acknowledged pro. Yet on average Dee won about forty percent of the time. Those games in the forty percent rather intrigued Ed, and both men maintained a genuine interest in their games.

There was a knock on the door -- Dee never rang the bell. Upon opening the door there stood a beaming Dee with a six pack in his left hand. Dee delivered his ritual greeting; "How fares the friend?", and the ritual response followed, "All goes well." Ed was an informal soul, and in the early days Dee went to much effort to educate him and get him up to the mark; but on certain matters of decorum Dee was inflexible, and Ed eventually just made the 'correct' response and quit protesting.

As Dee ice boxed his six pack Ed got down to business; "Indulge a friend, Dee. Usually we have a beer and visit, then play chess; this evening I want to start with chess. Also, I want to switch the stakes: If I win you can stay home Saturday night, while if you win you must go."

"Sure Ed; I have no objections, but it is a curious suggestion. Any particular reasons?"

Ed smiled mysteriously, "There are reasons within reasons, which I will share with our after-chess beer."

"Good, and I mean to refresh your memory on that point; your reasons are always deep and interesting -- for a mathematical type."

The men set up the board and got right down to it. An hour and a half later, after an unusually intricate game in which Ed could find nothing specific to regret, it was determined Dee would be attending the welcoming party.

In the post game beer moment, as a thoughtful and rather pleased Ed was screwing the top off his bottle, Dee did indeed refresh his memory.

"Okay Ed, why did you switch the wager around? The first wager made sense: you wanted me at the party and played for the party, while I wanted a quiet night at home and played for same. The second wager made no sense; why would you propose it?"

Ed positively beamed at Dee; "Dee, our game strongly suggests factor X has momentum-like properties: how does that grab you?!"

Dee was nonplussed; "I feel more perplexed than grabbed. What is factor X?"

So Ed proceeded to cite the many instances of preposterously favoring coincidence. As he talked Dee grew quiet and thoughtful. Ed concluded with a summary of their recent game.

"Dee, there is gigantic scope for coincidence in a chess game and when I proposed the wager twenty-four hours ago I would have bet money on your winning tonight, just like you did. However, at the last moment we switched the stakes, yet, even though 'winning' is now losing, you won the game, despite my playing very good chess. So I conclude, factor X has momentum; it can't stop or redirect on a dime.'

Ed paused; "Remember, Dee, you literary types hanker after essences and the suchness of experience. We physical science types are very different; we study behavior, and may or might not posit theoretical entities to make sense of it. You, I suspect, know factor X the way you know the warm sun on your back, whereas I merely know it has momentum."

Ed was secretly hoping Dee would 'open up', astound him with revelations and things never heard before. Instead.

"Ed, I feel young again! This is as good and exciting as solving the mysteries of creation in graduate school. You are wasted in Math; a man who can do what you've done with mere coincidence and luck should work on the great American novel.'

Dee paused; "I suppose you were being far too creative to have read the Canadian author I recommended; remember, Robertson Davies?"

Ed was sheepish; "You are right, Dee; I didn't get my homework done. This week without fail. But don't forget tonight's little lesson; coincidence, or mere luck, has momentum.

A Rainy Day

He turned back to it for the third time; "As perplexed as an explorer from sunless lands puzzling over an ancient sundial taken from ruins which orbit a star." This was truly a disturbing thought; you might know yourself to be clueless without ever suspecting what vast, stygian depths the word hides. So clueless a kindly offered explanation possesses no handholds, no words or experience upon which to hang one's understanding; akin to explaining tennis or a Mozart quartet to an amoeba.

That was the deeper puzzle; when to suspect there is no explanation of the desired and assumed kind, that one is an amoeba puzzling over tennis. In a word, recognizing your true situation.

He put the book back on the slightly dusty shelf and continued down the stack. He browsed in a leisurely and thoughtful way, fully aware there was no place he'd rather be on a wet rainy fall day than in an old used book store.

He reached the end of the row when an old clock chimed the hour. He was supposed to meet Ann for lunch!

He fetched his umbrella from the stand in the front of the store, nodded pleasantly to the proprietor, and hurried out to the wet cobblestones. He turned right and walked quickly up the street; their little lunch nook was close and he would be at most a few minutes late, or, happy thought, Ann would be late and he could play the righteous one!

He happened to look across the street and came to a confused stop; there, between the library and Sam's Emporium, was the entrance to the park with the tree! But Sam's Emporium and the library were immediately adjacent and the park was miles away!!

As he was starting across the street to investigate, the silver bell chimed; lunch with Ann, and the park with the tree were good things, but the silver bell chimed in yet better, and furthermore he had no choice in the matter.

The chimes had not yet died when he found himself attired in more formal clothes looking over twenty to thirty young adults whose attentive faces were all focused on him. He paused significantly, gathered them with his eye, then embarked boldly and with enthusiasm to share what he knew and loved of life and its intricate and multifarious details. He paced the room as he talked, and he held them spellbound for near an hour. Too soon the chime sounded, and again he found himself back on the cobblestone street holding an umbrella to keep the weather off; yes, he was back, and soon hurrying to his lunch date with his wife Ann. This was the way of time between the chimes, it was 'off the clock' and never caused the slightest problem.

Soon after arriving at the Purple Onion he realized he'd arrived before Ann; perfect! He had barely ordered coffee before in she bustled, rosy cheeked with the fall weather, and flustered at losing track of time.

After a tasty and pleasant lunch they yet again divided to conquer, he to visit another old book store, she to visit several last shops. His way passed the library and Sam's Emporium, and they were as they always were, immediately adjacent; the earlier moment was evidently an odd and passing fancy.

After the Party

It was quite early Sunday morning and Ed and Kim had at least an hour before the kids were up and about. They sipped their coffee in companionable silence. As they looked out the window of the breakfast nook two humming birds were at the new feeder. Their pattern was to sip a few seconds, withdraw, sip a few seconds, withdraw. There were no other birds or animals in sight and this struck Ed as an excessively strenuous way to break one's fast. However, be as that may, their wings were an iridescent blur in the morning sunshine and the scene was charming. At length Kim broke the Sabbath peace.

"Well, Ed, what did you think of the new couple?"

Ed took a thoughtful sip before answering; "They look like a solid addition to our faculty. Joshua is a striking specimen of a man; looks like a mix of a film star and a top level athlete. I hear he is second to none as a lecturer. The wife, Miri, is not so striking, but seemed okay."

Kim chuckled; "I know someone who would reverse your assessment."

"Actually, so do I; was Dee so very transparent!?"

Kim hesitated, "Yes, Ed, he was. When he saw Miri across the room he reminded me of a hunting dog coming to 'point'. The rest of the evening he played moth to her flame. In its way the whole business was something of a revelation; I have never seen Dee take much interest in any particular woman, and I never realized he could be so very, very, charming."

"The odd thing, Kim, is there seemed to be an answering fire; a flow of soul, deep calling to deep, that sort of thing.

The whole business is jarring, out of character; I hope I don't come to regret dragging him to the party."

Ed trailed off into silence, then, just as his wife was about to speak; "We are probably safe; Professor Miri Kirkwood seems pretty ordinary to me, and this encourages one to hope Dee will return to baseline. You're the thoughtful student of people, Kim; any thoughts?"

Kim <u>was</u> a thoughtful student of her fellow man and had been a practicing Jungian therapist until sidetracked by Ed's gallantry; "I hope you are right, Ed, but it had better not depend on Miri being ordinary, because she's not. What is ordinary, best of men, is your perception."

Skiing

He adjusted his dark glasses, got a good grip on his poles, and gave a mighty push down the slope. Like a hunting falcon stooping for its prey he swooped down on Ann, who was a quarter mile lower. He pulled up just above her and laid a wall of powder over her.

After Ann shook the snow off her ski cap and glasses she said; "Okay, Jay; your choice."

"How frisky you feeling?"

Ann considered; "Frisky enough; but if you end up at the midmountain chalet for lunch then I'm friskisima."

"So, its friskisima you feel, wench? I'll fix that!"

He left the official way and into scattered trees and a steeper slope. The way chosen was challenging spiced with danger, but both were excellent skiers and they arrived mid mountain weary but exuberant.

After a leisurely lunch they skied the other side of the mountain, mostly on single black diamond runs; double blacks were for morning skiing. Just before 4 P.M. they were coasting down a low lying 'green' slope headed for home. The green soon gave way to a gently descending trail through the woods. A quarter mile from home the trail divided. Jay recognized the branch leading home but was surprised the other branch was the familiar trail to the little park.

He hadn't visited the park in a while and now found he wanted to visit it; the wish was unexpectedly strong, which rather surprised him.

"Ann, let's go to the park; just for five to ten minutes."

"Jay, I don't like the park; somehow it frighten me, puts me off. Besides, tonight's special and I'm cooking something new. You go, and I'll head home and start cooking. Take your time; dinner won't be ready for one and a half to two hours."

Ann matched the deed to the thought and Jay found himself alone at the bifurcation. He started towards the park.

Jay had never entered the park during winter so he was quite surprised to pass from winter to late summer within twenty feet. Instead of snow there was a carefully wrought flagstone path which passed amongst trees in full summer leaves and a lovely vibrant lawn. This had immediate practical consequences; he took off his skis and leaned them and his poles against a convenient tree, then loosened his boots.

Within several hundred yards the path opened into the park itself, which was circular in shape with a diameter of about one hundred eighty feet. There were maples and pines around the margins, and just back of the trees stood a low stone wall enclosing the park. Lovely lawn stretched across the park, and, remarkably, was equally luxuriant under the trees and more centrally where it communed directly with the sun.

In the center of the park stood an unusual fruit tree about forty feet tall, and forty feet from it there was a fountain. Between the tree and fountain, in the very middle of the park was an ordinary park bench. The flagstone path led to the bench and as it approached the bench it widened to include, with some margin, both the bench and the fountain. The tree stood back from the flagstones on the lawn; around the immediate perimeter of the tree was a margin of Lily of the Valley.

Thus far Ann, or, for that matter, anyone else, found the park charming. It was only as one sat on the central bench things grew odd; so seated one was simultaneously in two very different scenes.

To one's left, facing the fountain, it was a very clear and still autumn evening, with stars so sharp and bright you could cut diamonds with them. The fountain was become an entrancing play of light and water, with the light varying across the entire spectrum of color and mixing in an exquisite music with the mist, spray, and fountain. The fountain had the unusual property that its fascination never palled, never faded; an hour later one sat as entranced as during the early moments. It was a thing of unalloyed charm and peace.

When one turned right, towards the tree, it was a windy mid afternoon late summer day with scudding clouds, but no hint of rain or storm. It was an invigorating, good day to be walking. The leaves of the tree rustled in the breeze and the brownish-maroon fruit swayed where it hung, but never fell. In large black print against a light gray background was a sign with no visible means of support; it just was there, unconnected to either heaven or earth. The sign read:

The Tree of Knowledge of Good and Evil

Be thrice warned: If this fruit be eaten everything will change. Once eaten there is no return to this bench and life as ye know it. The new path, as certain as the pull of Mother Earth, will exact toil, sorrow, and pang. But there is the chance of climbing, and some who climb will see the world grow larger, stranger, and more beautiful.

Ann found sitting on the bench thoroughly disturbing, and after a few times avoided the park. For Jay it was otherwise, and he could have passed a lifetime watching the fountain. He spent much less time on the windy afternoon, and this for a very simple reason; the story of Oedipus.

Upon coming across the story in high school literature, and ever since, he had always found Oedipus a fathead's fathead. Oedipus had sat on this very bench, eaten of the fruit, and a lot of good it did him! Recognize a good thing, and don't 'rock the boat'. Today, however, Jay's take on that distant reading was a little different. He thought of Oedipus' life before he ate the fruit. He felt pretty sure Thebes was not locked in a death struggle with plague or another city -- there would be neither time nor attention for playing with fruit. Oedipus was probably in the middle of a long, long comfortable stretch of coasting. What if he was by nature a climber? Of course ever mother's son of us likes coasting <u>and</u> climbing, each defines and reinforces the other. It would be a question of where they balanced for a given individual. The balance, for Oedipus of Thebes, had not been congenial.

So, Oedipus was predisposed, inclined, to eat the fruit, roll the dice; look where it got him! Full circle back to the fathead of the world -- and Jay turned back to the fountain. But seeds had been planted.

Thulas I

Ed and Dee had missed the last Thursday, as Ed's in-laws were in town. Now they were back on track, and as Ed strolled the several blocks to Dee's house he was keen and his step light.

There were two reasons for the light step. Firstly, he hadn't seen Dee for two weeks, and secondly, on the last occasion he had been unexpectedly ambushed and mauled; being beaten was tolerable, but ambushed and mauled?! Never! Ed's blood as a chess master was risen.

The evening started, as usual, with a social beer on the backyard deck.

Ed passed along what he'd been hearing; "Young Kirkwood seems to be even better than his reputation; his first lectures were riveting, memorable, and he seems to get on well with his peers in the department. In an appropriate, low key way, he is already trying to organize them towards a research project he has in mind."

Dee had heard such stories before; "If he is smart he'll tread softly; I'm pretty sure the lads in biology are more oriented towards their teaching duties and pay checks than pushing back the frontiers."

"No doubt, and if so, they are neither more nor less than the rest of us."

They drank in a companionable silence, then Ed picked up where he'd left off; "Dee, that last remark wasn't entirely fair; haven't you written two highly regarded books, one on the critics true task, and the other on 18th century writers and their cultural background and mindset?"

"True, Ed, and thanks for noting these modest achievements, but both are downstream a bit, and for the last decade I have been more focused on my pay check and keeping my teaching obligations minimal; I am become a creature of the trough and status quo. This may change soon; we'll see."

"How's <u>your</u> professor Kirkwood doing, Dee?"

"Miri is doing well enough; she isn't, and won't ever be a brilliant lecturer. While this is so, it is balanced by her literary judgment, which, as best I can tell, is remarkable. She gets on well with peers and students and seems to be fitting in nicely."

"It seems young Joshua is the rising star and the one to watch", observed Ed.

"So it would seem", agreed Dee.

They passed to other things and ten minutes later sat down to chess. Ed proved irresistible, even magnificent, and before the hour was up Dee's king was carried away in chains.

As they were putting away the chess game, Ed, flush with victory and several earlier beers, unloaded a background fret and concern.

"Remember the welcoming party for the Kirkwood's, Dee? What was it, three of four weeks ago? Well, you seemed besotted with Miri Kirkwood, and it rather alarmed Kim and myself. It sounds as though you have recovered your equilibrium and are safely past a potential bog."

Dee positively beamed; "Ed, you bring back a wonderful memory; that was an incomparable evening, and I owe it all to you, even if you contrived it to show good fortune has momentum. I was and am besotted with Miri. Miri is that rarest of rare treasures, a thula, and I haven't seen one in years and years. Not only a thula, but such a thula! My interest and attraction for Miri will never 'blow over'; finally, she is one of life's oasis, not a bog. Mark my words, Ed, in six months Miri and I will be tight as ticks."

These remarks, so unlike Dee, were manifestly sincere, and so filled with headache and sorrow for all concerned that Ed, in something of a daze sank into a nearby chair.

"Wow, Dee; I don't know where to begin."

Dee was flattered at his friend's concern; "Ed, you anticipate a certain natural history and see trouble for the Kirkwoods, friend Dee, and the university ; sit back and relax, this business is heading towards a very different port, a port you cannot anticipate but will recognize when it arrives. Not to fret."

Ed was not consoled; "Dee, you are no comfort, rather you sound like a man who leaps off a cliff and assures friends he will be arriving some place other than the rocks below."

The friends sat in a companionable but rather glum silence. At length, more to get things back on track, Ed broke the silence; "Well, if I'm to have a comfortable ringside seat to the upcoming drama perhaps you'd better clue me into thulas; what on earth is a thula?!"

"That's the spirit, Ed!", Dee was visibly relieved, and then grew abstracted and thoughtful.

"Ed, I will do my best, but I'm in the position of describing ice cream to a person who has never been near ice cream. Thulas are perceived as very equable, even placid; their emotional range, rather them venturing far above and below baseline, is played out much closer to baseline, and in consequence their expressions are exquisite and subtle rather than color bombs. A thula startled, embarrassed, angry or rejoicing, may pass entirely unnoticed to the casual hick, but to the trained eye these moments are magical, delightful. Thulas are rather like a bonzai garden; details that pass unnoticed in a standard sized tree are easily and delightfully apparent in the miniature edition. Emotional range and its expression have interesting variations by race; facial expressions are particularly subtle and hard to detect in Chinese thulas - but all the more delightful when detected. Body language is a little richer in black thulas."

Ed was curious; "And white thulas such as Miri, any stronger suites?".

Dee smiled, happy with this sort of interruption, for he loved Thulas. "Of course, Ed, especially in northern Europe: their eyes. When we say the eyes of Asian and black women are dark we have spoken usefully, accurately, and have exhausted the subject. When we call the Nordic eye green, blue, brown, or dark we have neglected so much detail as to be almost misleading. Take Miri's eyes. At a best first approximation the least misleading thing is to call them blue, but when observed more closely one finds a dark, dark blue with an odd flame-like distribution. Look yet closer and one sees, swimming in the blue fire, graceful hunter green minnows. The more one looks the more is found and the upshot is a growing sense of the inadequacy and limitation of 'blue eyes.' These wonderful eyes are an important component of a white thulas 'bonsai garden."

Dee paused thoughtfully; "That covers the easy and immediate first impression; what follows is harder to define, and if you find it poor, confusing, and inadequate then rest assured, so do I."

"A thula has an approximate equipoise between three separate factors: deep roots in life, femininity, and intellect. By 'intellect' I mean a significant urge and effort to get life adequately reflected in language and to weigh and ponder that reflection. All three of these factors are strong and real in a thula, and no single factor, if you are to have a genuine thula, can significantly predominate.'

"The roots are so deep and strong they anchor and center a thula in a quite characteristic way. Thulas are deep wells of meaning and reassurance for those near them. Thulas are never overwhelmed, subsumed, or swept away in causes. At best they are tolerant of causes because those near and dear are swept away. Because of their viewpoint and intellect no one sees the edges and limitation of the various causes so well as a thula. Thulas seem self-sufficient and centered and this can be confused with self-centered narcissism. The narcissist is the center of all things, which is wherever they happen to be; thulas are deeply rooted from birth in the true center of things, and this cannot in the nature of things wander hither and thither.

"Lastly friend Ed, we come to femininity; in our day and age this is something of a tiger pit, and is the likeliest source of overlooking and missing a thula.'

"In the next few months Kim, strong daughter of Carl Jung, will with great authority be assuring you Miri is an ambulating pile of anima hooks and I am projecting various bits and pieces of myself on each and every hook. She will be completely wrong, but will have much plausibility."

Dee stopped and looked at Ed, and he had a twinkle in his eye; "Ed, no kidding, this really is coming and I am warning you not to arm you with arguments against Kim's view, after all, a smart husband would tell her how very sagacious she is, but that you should not be misled.'

"Thulas are <u>very</u> feminine, and very equable - to the point of appearing to almost lack affect; how can they escape the charge of ambulating anima hooks?! The difference between a thula and the vague feminine creatures Carl Jung dragged into the sunshine of a brighter day can be subtle to the casual eye, but are night and day to the experienced eye. 'Anima hooks' are to be found on thulas, but it is incidental to what a thula is, which is a deeply rooted woman of intellect. Carl Jung's targets are essentially and predominately anima hooks; there is little independent substance."

"So much for the verbal reflection of a thula, Ed; you, lucky man, shall have the real article in which to rejoice and reflect."

"I hope so,' was the noncommittal response; 'Now, where does the word 'Thula' come from?"

Dee smiled enigmatically; "It's an old literary term that wouldn't interest a mathematician like yourself."

"Ah; so you've forgotten. A final point; how can you be so sure six months from now you will be tight as a tick with Miri? Is this wishful thinking? After all, her husband is like a greek god and you're old enough to be her - uncle?"

"Ed, my lad, be made aware we literary types, around women, have hidden depths. It will be so."

Later in the evening, back home, Ed tried to find 'Thula,' in the dictionary, and drew a blank. It was only years later he came to realize just how ancient thulas and their mystique were.

An Evening of Bridge With Friends

Ann organized and laid her hand down opposite Jay, then, since she was the 'dummy,' she smiled encouragingly and left to make the Irish coffees. The prospect of Irish coffees was pleasant to all; after all, cool autumn evenings were made for Irish coffees. Yet even this imminent cheer and balm could not dent Jay's sense of numb incredulity; how, how, could he and Ann have bid these hands to game level?! He opened with hearts, but only by the skin of this teeth. Ann replied with two clubs, and this was more to make some response to what she must have imagined was vast strength in hearts; ten points and four clubs, queen high, was hardly towering strength. He, knowing his 'one heart' for the weak creature it was, desperately returned with three clubs, she, equally desperate to be clear of clubs put them at three hearts.

So, here he was, the Egyptian hosts approaching, and somehow he had to part the red sea and escape to safety. The central question; should be play to minimize loss, or play to win? Was winning possible? He reviewed the bidding, and thought of the cards out against him; was there a distribution consistent with the bidding where he might finesse his way to game?

Jay thought hard and quickly, he tried this, he tried that, he, aha! No...yes! But the odds, miserable thing, were whatever came after astronomical. Jay decided to play to win, and if his efforts went south he'd create a new, galactic type depth to what losing meant.

Two hours later as he and Ann walked home, rather Ann walked and he floated, he thought he knew how Moses felt as he led this people through the divided sea to safety.

The Plan

The doorbell rang, Dee opened the door, there stood Ed, but his ritual greeting 'How fares the friend' died abourning; "Damn, Ed, you're wasting away; down to skin and bones!"

As with all fat fighters, Ed was delighted -- someone had noticed.

"Thanks, Dee. What you aren't seeing is the steel in my legs; I'm running three miles every morning. Remember? I started with a half mile waddle."

In point of fact Dee <u>had</u> forgotten; "Ed, as human beings we have an understood obligation to wage war on middle age fat; but what is it with the running?"

"This may surprise you, Ed, but remember that six mile cross country race two months ago?"

"I do; barely. What of it? This race has never stirred you, lo, these many years; why now?"

"As you know, Scott Brennan owns the race. He was our cross country star five years ago and, though graduated, he returns to the alma mater every year for the autumn invitational cross country race. Well, not this year; an old fart gave him a paddling, care to guess?"

"Miri told me; Josh beat him by a few yards. By all reports it was quite a race. Josh not only looks an athlete, but is the real article; Miri was very proud. How did this launch you?"

"I don't really know, Dee, but it did. Something about Josh's indomitable spirit as a competitor stirred me; he came up from far back at the very end, and as he started that last kick I knew in my bones he was going to win, which, of course, he did. It was very exciting."

It was too cool for having the social beer outside, but they had made their way to the kitchen and were comfortably seated.

Ed chuckled; "Do you know what I see most mornings as I puff my way along the three miles?"

"An unbodied joy whose race has just begun?"

Ed caught the allusion, and was quite pleased; "No, P. Shelley; I see you and Miri. You two are so intent on your talk I don't believe you notice me, or much else, for that matter. Is it entirely due to thula magic, or are you two up to something?"

"We are up to something, and I think it is going to be very, very good."

Dee paused, took a swig, and was getting ready to leave the topic of 'something good'.

"None of that, Dee. What are you up to?"

"Okay, Ed; you're the bosom friend so I will share, but as of yet Miri doesn't know my aim so this is for your ears only.

"Months ago I told you Miri would never make much of a stir as a lecturer, or, to be truthful, as a teacher. I want her career secure and independent of her brilliant husband. Remember what I said? When it comes to books and literature she is the real article; she has a wonderful nose and feel for what is genuinely good. Currently we are reading through the good popular literature of the second half of the twentieth century, the books of Herman Hesse, Kurt Vonnegut, Douglas Adams, Tolkien and many others. We read the same book, and then thoughtfully discuss, and slowly one by one we are getting through our list. We read in the evening and discuss on the early morning walk.'

Dee paused, then, a smile, "Sharing with a sympathetic 'new' person breathes youth and life into things old and worn; our morning walks are wonderfully, magically exhilarating. I am keeping careful notes on our talks and soon we will write several books with Miri as first author; these books will be very good, and her professional well-being will be firmly anchored."

Ed was both charmed and a little surprised; "It is good of you to look out for her, Dee, but solid mediocrity isn't so bad; most of us are in that camp and get by. Is there something you have omitted to tell? Something that makes you a little uneasy on her behalf?"

"There is, and there isn't. As you know, there are far more young professors of English literature than there are positions available -- universities are very much in a position to pick and choose, so the wise professor tries to distinguish herself from the pack.'

"Now for the inside scoop; our department really didn't need a professor, but biology wanted Josh, wanted him so much, in fact, that we made room for Miri. In the English department no one is being overworked so this is a good time for Miri to buff up the CV."

Ed was curious. "What exactly do you have in mind, Dee?"

"You know my views, Ed; I wouldn't write the time of day for a specialist academic audience. I only and always address the educated general reader who has a thoughtful turn. Miri doesn't yet realize our goal, but we will write to and for thoughtful readers in their late fifties and sixties and it will be a review and assessment of the books that delighted and molded us, that were 'in the air' in our university days and professional life. I would gladly buy and read such a book, and there must be others. Miri will be perfect for this project and I will be her midwife."

"Have you got a title in mind?"

"An Experienced Reader Looks Back, or An Older Reader Looks Back, or perhaps A Thoughtful Reader Looks Back; you decide Ed."

Ed laughed; "Mr. Belushi is offering cheeseburgers, or cheeseburgers. Shaping Books of the Boomers; An Older Reader Looks Back. There it is, Dee; take it or leave it."

"I'll take it under consideration. Now Ed, old buddy, if you are not too frightened, how about some chess; I promise to take it easy on you."

"That's grand of you, Dee; when it comes to chess you are a frightening tower of strength, but there is something that scares at least as much, perhaps more."

Ed was grown quite serious and Dee knew exactly what ailed him.

"Ed, you are about to echo Kim's concerns; Miri and I are too much together and seem to enjoy ourselves too much. Might something be in play beneath the surface; slap and tickle perhaps? Well, take your imagination off the stove; our behavior is as proper and pure as fresh fallen snow. Josh is very busy and focused on various projects in his department and is, if anything, pleased and grateful his wife is happy and occupied. This will change; there will come a time when he will see himself as having the mammalian and domestic side of his wife while I have the woman's heart. This will never be true, but in time it will be true enough. However their marriage now and forever has no more faithful friend and protector than myself. All proceeds as it will and must; you were, if I recall correctly, to sit back and watch a curious and different story develop. No fretting, not even a hint of fret. Now, what is to be: chess or fretting?! Remember Ed, I can't and won't be a source of fretting and sleeplessness in people I truly count as friends."

Unaccountably, Ed took this counsel; going forward he made it a point to lay aside worry on behalf of Dee. If Dee jumped off a cliff assuring some destination other than the rocks below then so be it. It proved wonderful training for his sons, who would be teenagers soon.

The Sea Shore

Jay and Ann were having a breakfast out on the screened in porch. It was an early summer morning and until recently it would have been too cool for a shirt sleeve breakfast on the porch, but today it was perfect; the porch was back for the summer, and would soon be the center of operations.

Jay was reaching for another forkful of bacon and eggs when the silver bell chimed and Jay found himself in a well appointed room standing beside a long table around which were six middle aged men and a woman; he had the undivided attention of everyone at the table. Like a rapidly rising tide the background and details of the scene engulfed him; he grasped them firmly, and began.

An hour later the silver bell chimed and once again his fork was descending towards the bacon and eggs. As always, Jay, found silver bell time wonderfully invigorating, and he greatly enjoyed his breakfast.

After putting away the breakfast things, Ann kissed him goodbye and left for an outing with her mother. Jay got his day pack, a light lunch, a towel, a mask, a bottle of water, and in the event fortune favored him, a few specimen bottles. The day was cool, sunny, and breezy; perfect for his expedition. Jay knew a lovely side path to the seashore and soon the maples and oaks gave way to small pines, then hardy shrubs and grass, and finally a rocky seashore that was like the coast of Maine, only a little more rugged. Not now or at any time did it strike Jay as odd all the best things of life should be a comfortable walk from his lovely home; this was merely life as he found it.

Jay was like a ten year old boy amongst the rocks and had a great time leaping his way along the coast. He saw an albatross, which was equally charming and surprising -- an albatross is rarely seen so close to shore. Another surprise was a good sized octopus trapped in a tidal pool; evenso Jay would not have seen it had he not ventured quite far out on a tenuous archipelago of scattered rocks. There were an abundance of crabs, sea anemones, and a few sea urchins.

Jay arrived at a large rock well out from shore and decided to have his lunch. He was opening his pack to get his lunch when a flash of dull red caught his attention; near his rock, in about eight feet of water, was not one, but two husky lobsters. Jay stripped, donned his mask, and with spartan fortitude jumped into the cold water; he returned to his rock in triumph and with supper. While the lobsters reviewed their situation from within his pack Jay had lunch and rapidly dried in the sea breezes and sunshine; Ann was in for a treat tonight!

Jay left his shirt off and as he made his way back along the coast the sun felt good on his back. The sounds of the seashore, the waxing and ebbing sound of the surf on the rocks, always congenial to Jay's ear, on this trip had an usual outcome; the seashore and its sounds turned Jay's thoughts to the tree and the fountain, especially the tree. There may come a time in a man's life when everything directs one's attention towards the tree, but that's as may be; certain it was that today the sounds of the sea brought the tree to mind. As Jay pondered the tree and the warning against eating its fruit he came face to face with a niggling, ghostly thought at the back of his mind; why did Ann shy away from the park? For shy she did; of late there was always some reason why she needed to stay home and he should visit the park alone. He and Ann were closer than close; he'd need to remember to ask her, and she would tell her story.

Celebrating

Josh and Miri had been at the university twenty months. Josh was more than ever the rising young star, the man to watch. His research plans were being implemented and his success as a teacher and lecturer would be hard to overestimate. Also, as predicted by Dee, he was becoming aware Miri's center of being did not seem with him and their home, but rather with Dee and their literary project. He doubted he was a cuckold, at least in the simple sense, but more and more he was aware of background talk, and he didn't like it. More and more he found himself irritated with Dee, like a low grade blister.

Three months earlier <u>Boomers and Their Books</u> had been published and, while hardly rivaling Stephen King, it was doing much better than expected and had been well received by the reviewers and critics. These are good things, but equally important is that both Dee and Miri liked their book and felt it reflected their discussions gracefully and well.

To commemorate and celebrate <u>Boomers and Their Books</u> Ed and Kim were having a party, which was off to a lively start. Ed, Kim, Miri, and Shelley, a friend of Kim's, were in the kitchen while Dee, Josh, and Tom Silva, an English department colleague of Dee's, were in the front room; lively conversations engaged both rooms. The conversation of Tom, Dee, and Josh concerned a man's margins and when a self identity has been irreparably fractured. Dee, with considerable plausibility and art, was arguing there was no such thing as an irreparable fracture. Josh, with surprising acumen and subtlety for a scientific type, argued irreparable fractures <u>were</u> possible, and happened in real life, but often they were not seen for what they were till ten plus years later. Such events were not yet another incident in a certain kind of story, but rather marked the end of one kind of story and the beginning of another kind of story. Tom Silva, seeking clarity, asked for a specific example.

"I cannot speak for another man, but if I killed a friend in full awareness of my act and without clear cut mitigating circumstances I would have crossed such a line, whether or not I was aware of it at the time."

Dee looked both impressed and thoughtful; "Josh, I will concede the field to you; that was strongly and well put. May I ask a favor?"

Josh might find Dee irritating, but Dee was unquestionably a strong friend and help to his wife, who, Josh was quite certain, would never have made her way into print on her own.

"Sure, Dee; as you literary types like to say, unto the half of my kingdom."

"The other day Ed and I were discussing a similar topic, and your remark closes the matter so succinctly and well I would like you to repeat your last thought for him, and please, verbatim, exactly as given."

Whereupon Dee left his chair, dragged a puzzled Ed away from his own conversation, and whispered as they left the room, "Ed, this is important; Josh is going to repeat to you something he just told Tom and me. Mark his words closely, and tell him how well put they are."

Josh was a little embarrassed; "Sorry for the interruption, Ed. Dee thinks my last sentence so golden you must hear it."

Dee gave a background précis, after which Josh shared his own fracture point. Ed was attentive, appreciative, and deeply puzzled.

Ann and The Tree

The lobster for which you have ventured and suffered much taste best and Jay was thinking that never in the history of the world had there been such lobsters as these charmers he'd brought home to Ann; mercy, but they tasted, what?! Sublime? Sublime should reach so high!

Towards the end rational thought again became possible; "Ann, why are you put off by the tree beside the fountain? Can you explain it to me?"

A surprised and suddenly serious, hard look came over Ann's face; "Jay, I am surprised you should ask me about your damn tree. If it is candor you want I'll give you an earful, but candor, unlike ice cream, rarely goes well with apple pie, and I have great hopes for mine; leave it till after supper."

'What bee is stinging her bottom?', wondered Jay; but for the nonce he put the matter aside.

When the last pie crumbs were gone Jay returned to the tree; "Ann, why are you touchy about the tree?"

Ann was exasperated; "Jay, there is no tree! Why do you go on about it so?! This is not like you; it's more like your brother, who is such a leg puller I never know when he's kidding and when he's serious. This tree business is not at all like you, and it is frightening. Also I can't get used to turning right and finding a windy summer day, and then turning left to find a starry night. Like you I find the fountain and lights very beautiful, but it doesn't begin to compensate a contemporaneous summer day and my husband acting so strangely. Why? Why?! Why?!!"

Jay was stunned; "Ann, sweetheart, I'm exactly the man you married; I'm not playing at some devious prank: the tree is really there. What do you see as you turn to the right?!"

"Jay, what I see, really and truly, is a lovely green lawn that extends to the trees on the margin of the park. Nothing else; no tree, no lily of the valley, no sign hanging unsupported between heaven and Earth: just lawn, lawn, and more lawn!"

"Okay, sweetie; I believe you. But it is equally certain I am seeing a tree. Tomorrow we'll visit the park and try to resolve the problem."

The next morning after breakfast they walked to the park. He and Ann approached the tree; Jay could no more walk through the tree than he could jump the moon, for Ann it was different; she did not see any tree and could, apparently, walk right through it. Jay picked a fruit, which was cool and firm to touch. He put the fruit in Ann's hand and it went right through her hand and fell to the ground; she neither saw nor felt the fruit. There was something exceeding strange in Ann's interactions with the tree; neither the tree nor it's fruit were a ghostly background to Ann, nor Ann a ghostly background to the tree or fruit. Both Ann and the tree, when superimposed, remained distinctly themselves, and in conjunction had an appearance so strange Jay almost had to pinch himself. Ann and the tree were like quantum states, equally real and equally unreal.

He was on his own when it came to the tree; it wasn't there for Ann.

There was a last surprise. When finished with the fruit Jay, who had a throwing arm second to none, gave it a mighty toss that should have sent it far beyond the park. Instead it flew rapidly away and then just disappeared. When Jay turned around it was back in place and the tree appeared untouched.

Working on the Second Book

Heinlein's <u>Stranger in a Strange Land</u> brought the questing friends into a swamp of perplexity; the prose, quo prose, was pretty ordinary, while the 'message' was vague; more hopeful and silly than anything else. But of course that was just the point; Heinlein's book surfed the wave of the sixties, a wave notably vague, hopeful, and silly.

As they turned into the Kirkwood's driveway Miri summarized; "Dee, great literature creates its own wave and rides it grandly and forever. The really second rate stuff catches no waves of any kind. Stranger in Strange Land is somewhere in the middle and has handles for waves. The 'handle' is probably the clever story that gives India and Tibet a much needed rest and drafts the Martians as the well of wisdom."

"Well put, Miri; and we'll need to recreate as best we can what a prophetic and powerful voice it was at the time, which will take some doing. Can you 'grok' that?"

Miri smiled at the allusion; "I think so. Now, slow down, Dee, I need to get you Professor Sommer's essay on Herman Hesse and his <u>Steppenwolf</u>."

While Miri hurried off to look for Professor Sommers Dee stepped into the living room and discovered Josh cleaning a rifle.

"Good morning, Dee. Did you and Miri wrestle any sort of sense from <u>Stranger in a Strange Land</u>?"

"Not much, Josh, and that little hard-won. What's with the gun?"

"Deer season starts a week from tomorrow, and I'm getting ready."

"Do you have a place to hunt?"

"I think I'll try around the old quarry. I need to look the place over, think like a deer, and decide how to hunt the area. I usually get a deer."

"I have always meant to hunt deer and never seem to get around to it."

"Why would you wish to hunt, Dee? It's usually cold and dull work, no excitement or romance to it."

"I'm sure you're right, Josh, but in literature hunting is frequently featured, or alluded to, and I have always thought I should have some familiarity with it. Would you mind greatly if I tagged along? I promise not to be a bother."

In point of fact Josh did mind; he always hunted alone and Dee was by now something of a constant irritant. But he stood in the fellow's debt; Miri's recent book was a strong forward step for her, and more was to follow. 'Damn! How to avoid the man, hmm. Ah, yes!'

"I don't mind at all, Dee, happy to help, but there are a few preliminaries. Do you have any experience with guns?"

"I shot a .22 as a kid."

"Good, but a .270 is a different animal. I have a spare gun for you but you will need to get down to the shooting range and fire it enough to be comfortable with it. Also, you will need to buy or borrow warm camouflaged pants and coat; I would lend you some clothes, but they would be too large. You will need to get a license. Lastly, if Saturday after next is wet or colder than usual then I'm leaving you home -- I won't have your pneumonia on my conscience. Those are the conditions; think it over before committing. Unfortunately it entails much expense and bother for the privilege of being cold and bored."

"Your conditions are eminently reasonable, Josh. Get your spare gun now so I have more time to pick a convenient moment to get down to the rifle range."

Josh put a good face on his consternation, but inside he was fuming; 'I should have said, 'Sorry, nothing personal, Dee, but I hunt alone." A few minutes later Dee left the Kirkwood home with both a rifle and Professor Sommers. Josh was left praying for either a cold snap or rain, preferably both.

Wednesday evening, after their chess game a concerned Ed shared a thought.

"Dee, I hear you are going hunting with Josh; this is a bad idea. In case you have missed it, Josh doesn't like you, and doesn't wish good things for you. Make your excuses and bow out, please."

Dee was touched. "I appreciate the thought, Ed, but this is part of that spectacle at which you have a comfortable ringside seat. Remember; no fretting?"

Ed had a stray, dark thought; "Dee, surely you aren't planning anything unfortunate for Josh! He's a fine young man and his response to you is only to be expected."

"Shame on you, Ed! You know me better than that. I will never bring harm on Josh."

The Storm

The lightening was spectacular and lit up the entire evening countryside in a whitish rather ghostly day; the following thunder seemed to rattle the world. The driving sleet and rain were a relentless backdrop to the more dramatic lightening, but frequently strong gusts would move the rain into the foreground of Jay's awareness.

He and Ann had fallen asleep lying as spoons on a large comfortable couch with Ann on the outside. The fire rearranged itself amidst a small flurry of sparks and with a soft, muffled voice of complaint. The warmth felt good; it wasn't far above freezing. The summer was gone, no doubt.

On their audio system a pensive, reflective guitar made its masterly and lyrical way through Tarrega's Recuerdos de La Alhambra with the lovely music only intermittently obscured by gusts of storm. Jay hugged his warm wife closer and felt poignantly warm, secure, and loved. Circumstances had conspired to bring his blessings into the sharpest possible focus.

A Cold Evening Turns Warm

It was a cold evening with a light steady snowfall. Ed should have been home at his desk grading exams, not walking the neighborhood like Hamlet's ghost; and he should have worn a warmer jacket, but the cold wasn't registering with him. It was nearly four weeks since Dee's death, and the fact of the thing was beginning to sink in; Ed was sleeping a little better, but as of yet far from well, at most two to three hours at a stretch. Ed had a deep and abiding urge to understand, to sort things into useful and comprehensible patterns, and the circumstances of Dee's death were intractably strange; Ed craved sense, and there was no sense.

The ill fated hunting expedition with Josh ended with Dee falling to his death at least a hundred yards from where Josh had settled him to hunt. This was odd enough, but Dee had prepared carefully and in detail for his death. Ed received four hundred thousand in trusts for his two boys and two hundred thousand in stocks and bonds. One item brought a wry smile to Ed's careworn face; when the lawyer, with a laugh, handed Ed the $1.00 lottery ticket the honorable one viewed it as a thing cute and quaint; Ed saw it as close to five hundred thousand - which as of three days ago, it had become. There was a final surprise. Dee had a chess set which had been carved from ivory and was ancient; Dee spoke as though it came from the sixteenth century. A month before his death Dee asked Ed what he thought it worth, and Ed, in a burst of foolish extravagance, opined it might go as high as twenty thousand. Dee laughed, and said it would bring at least four hundred thousand. Dee then told Ed the set had been willed to Ed, under the condition it not be sold earlier than two months after Dee's death. Ed thought this a little morbid and out of character and promptly forgot it. A week ago he had heard back from Sotheby's that it was worth between four hundred and five hundred thousand. Ed and Dee always played with the ancient set and both men loved it; Ed did not intend to sell it, it was his link with his friend.

The remainder surprised everyone but Ed; Miri got the house and, excepting the chess set, everything in it, Dee's car, the small summer cottage, and two hundred thousand in cash. Dee's home was larger and nicer than the humbler Kirkwood digs and one week ago Josh and Miri put their house up for sale and moved to Dee's home.

The will strongly suggested Dee knew his death was imminent; was his death part of some plan, or was it a conceivable downside which Dee covered as best he could? With anyone but Dee this was the idlest of idle questions. And so poor Ed slipped into a weary and well worn groove of theory and speculation, and as always it led nowhere.

Ed was so preoccupied and the visibility so poor he almost ran into another, larger man. Ed looked up, and into the concerned face of Josh Kirkwood.

Josh said; "I don't need to ask 'How fares the friend.' I can see for myself; you're not faring so well, and you're cold. Here, put this on." He handed Ed a spare coat he was carrying.

Ed started to remonstrate but Josh ignored him and started to put the coat on him, whereupon Ed complied.

"Ed, by now you've received estimates on my old chess set; was I pretty close?"

Ed looked closely at Josh Kirkwood and a prolonged silence followed; then, "Dee?"

"Yes, I'm here."

Another silence; "So, Dee, I suppose this is more of your luck?"

"It is."

A longer silence; "Dee it frightens me more than I can say, but I must ask; what has become of Josh Kirkwood?"

"It is too cold to stand around like this; come, let's walk a bit."

As they started walking 'Josh' continued, "Josh is fine; in fact, he's in his very own paradise."

This brought Ed back completely from the numbing incredulity that had overtaken him since meeting Josh-Dee; "Dee, don't talk nonsense; answer the question head-on and fairly!"

"Ed, there's an older poet I rather like who told his lady love he would build her a palace of green days of forest and blue days at sea; I've done something like that for Josh. I have taken a hundred or so of his brightest and best memories, changed them slightly to make them yet brighter, and created a paradise for him. He is loved and happy. The dangerous and sporting part of it from my angle is that he can return to full possession of Joshua Kirkwood anytime he chooses."

"Dee, please, bear with me; can you make this paradise a little clearer?"

Dee thought awhile; "Perhaps. Imagine a beautiful, complex, stained glass window in a very fine cathedral, further imagine a bright but cloudy summer day. Each small portion of the window is one of the hundred or so memories; the sunlight is Josh's awareness, and due to the clouds and their unpredictable patterns the light never comes to the window quite the same way ever again - it's like a fire, or sunshine on water - eternally the same and eternally different."

"Yes, that's better. So it is pretty pleasant, is it?"

"Yes, Ed; really and truly, Josh is in paradise. However, humanity, especially the Joshes of our world, won't linger overly long amongst the lotus eaters. I should have about fifteen to twenty years before he exercises his freedom. So there is plenty of time for chess and other good things, things like Miri. Next week let's get back to Wednesday evening chess at my place - you'll need to lend me your chess set. One thing, Ed; you will need to watch yourself carefully for a few months: I'm Josh to Miri. I'm carefully titrating in 'Dee, but from now on Dee is gone and now and forever I'm Josh Kirkwood."

Ed was much recovered, and getting, as was Ed's way, curious; "Begging your pardon, Dee, but is Josh's choice to return, easy, a cousin to 'I'll have toast instead of buns'.

"No, it is very hard and very painful; it is Jim leaping from the deck of the Patna."

"Dee, I usually track your literary references pretty well, for example earlier your lotus eaters is from Tennyson's poem of the same name, but Jim and the Patna, while doubtlessly as apt and sharp as a new pin, eludes me."

"Sorry, Ed. Read Conrad's <u>Lord Jim</u>. When a high minded young idealist leaps from the Patna he is discovering he too is merely of clay; it can be a most desperately unhappy thought. In Josh's own words, 'a discontinuity of the self.'

"I take it Josh was something less than his best self on your hunting trip?"

"Yes, and no. For now I'm dropping the curtain on myself and the successful hunting trip. When my time grows short I'll tell you everything you want to know; from now till then we are just ordinary middle aged professors and friends making our way gently towards the grave. I see halcyon days ahead, Ed. It is enough to be alive and have friends such as yourself and Miri."

The Game

There was no time for thought, only lightening quick reactions; Jay feinted towards the left and with the inside of his left foot kicked the ball to his right. The feint was almost too good - it fooled the opposing forward - and Jay had trouble reversing his momentum. When he caught up with the ball there was barely time to get off a long lofting kick which brought the ball down in the vicinity of the opposing goal; with any luck one of the lads could head it in.

Skip caught the ball on his forehead but unfortunately it came off fast and at an angle very different than intended. Phooey! What?! A huge shout had erupted; they had scored!!

It was one of those flukes which keep sports forever green; the ball had ricocheted off the head of an opposing player and into the goal.

Jay was elated to the bursting point; what a game, what an impossible game! Ann had better have stayed attentive; damn, this was historical!

It really was 'historical'; before the game nobody would have ventured even a nickel on the 'Bolts', a good team of enthusiastic amateurs in a lightweight league of other sporting enthusiasts. The Tigers, by way of contrast, were a semiprofessional team. This exhibition game was, for the Tigers, an indulgence and a chance to paddle some beginners.

It had certainly started that way; in the first half it was 3-0, Tigers. In the second half something happened and the Bolts came alive to forge ahead with irresistible momentum; soon it was 3-3. At which point the Tigers defense became a stonewall and their offense exploded. Fortunately this happened near the end of the game and the Bolts, by a whisker, were holding them off and heading things into an overtime they would inevitably lose. Then, in the last seconds of the game, they triumphed by a fluke. The game wasn't David and Goliath, it was ant and lion.

After being kissed and told the game was 'historical', Ann left to spend the evening with her literary club while Jay walked home.

Sometime ago Jay had decided to roll the dye and eat the fruit. However, he wanted to leave, step off, from a mountain top; this afternoon was an Everest. He had never felt less like leaving, but the plan was a child of cooler, more thoughtful moments, and he'd stand by it; this evening he would eat the damn fruit.

Jay's decision had its roots in that odd moment on a rainy day when he'd been browsing through the old used bookstore. The old poem had alluded to men from a sunless world musing over an ancient sun dial. After long thought Jay decided his own balance between coasting and climbing lay beyond his control, beyond his world. This is a subtle thought in an area where certainty is not possible, but over time Jay had become certain enough.

Indeed, Jay would have left some time ago, but for an agonizing, poignant problem -- Ann.

Halcyon Days End

Evening was falling as Ed walked to Josh's home for their weekly chess game. It was early summer nine years and eight months since Dee's death.

Ed knocked on the door and was met by Josh, who was holding two cold beers. "The friend looks as though he is faring well and, putting a beer in Ed's hand, 'he is about to fare better."

"Miri's busy and I don't want to disturb or distract her; let's walk around to the deck and do the right thing by these cold lads."

When they were comfortably seated; "Ed, this is a special evening, and it's all yours; the original Josh is within a few days of returning, and it could be hours, though most likely not. I promised I would answer your questions when the end drew near; well, we're there."

"Josh, at our last conversation, many years gone by, you thought you had fifteen to twenty years; I don't think it has been ten years. You and Miri are started on a third very interesting book, Scott is a cutie and just about to start to school. Can you postpone things six or seven years?"

"I can and I can't; it is in my power, Ed, but for reasons that will soon be clear I am very strict about my rules. When you are cornered in chess it would often be extremely useful to change the rules, but this line of behavior would soon destroy chess. Josh Kirkwood will come or not come on his own schedule; that is how I play the game."

This was greeted with a thoughtful silence; "Damn, Josh, but I am going to miss you. Where will you go?"

"I will visit old friends awhile and then, most likely, pick up a drunk on skid row. I'll see."

"Josh, what on earth are you? You don't seem to be a standard issue human; are you some sort of a vampire?"

"A long time ago that was an easy question to answer: my origin precedes human origins and is very different. Now over many thousands of years I have come to see myself as human with a difference, sort of human plus."

"Josh, are you millions, or even billions of years old?"

"Misleading question, Ed. Your scientific extrapolations from a middle aged universe to an early, young universe wrong foots the issue. Early time is very, very different from middle age time and the middle age estimates are in consequence most misleading and miss the issue entirely. You are a mathematician, Ed and I have an analogy that may help. Imagine the origin is a straight line that your middle age time extrapolation is approaching at right angles. As you approach the line your extrapolation, without your being aware of it, deviates to the side and begins an asymptotic approach to the origin line. You are in a situation where many millions of years are estimated for very little real approach to the origin line."

"Is that how it works?" Ed was getting curious.

"No! It is emphatically not that way; you have been offered an analogy that may or may not be useful.'

"Think of the universe as a limb on the tree of existence with the central trunk being God. In the early days, the embryologic period, there is nonessential left over material that is neither trunk nor new limb. This 'material' in the nature of things must go either with the trunk or the new limb. To not be on the tree at all is nonexistence. About sixty percent of this material went back to the trunk, or God, while forty percent chose the new limb."

Josh paused, and gave Ed a wry smile; "You see, Ed, in terms of your mythology I'm one of the fallen angels."

Ed, in his youth, had frequented Sunday school; "Have you met an entity called Lucifer?"

"No, I have not. But joining the limb ultimately individuates us and takes us away from each other; there are no angelic clubs or social moments and we have long since changed and lost our status as angels quo angels. This was inherent in choosing to go with the limb."

"What has happened to the fallen angels, Josh; are they all like you?"

"They have, over the millennia, disappeared; I'm the last one. Time of the limb variety is a strange thing Ed. It is at the same time wonderfully quickening and terribly eroding. Time is the sandpaper of existence; eventually all is rubbed out and gone. Over seventy years in your own life a certain monotony and sameness appears; Josh Kirkwood, living in paradise, is ready to roll the die in less than a decade. Now imagine passing through millennia! My brothers are long, long gone.'

"Over the millennia all I find left for me, things that confer meaning and existence, are my rules, my friends, and thulas.

"Friends and thulas are not merely someone to sit by the winter fire with you, rather they are both the fire and the someone who sits by your side and talks with you. High minded ideals, contrary to popular thought, are, on the millennial scale, the first to go. Not that such things don't have a place, they do, but it is on the seventy year scale."

"All the dark angels may be gone, Josh, but according to popular culture and the movie industry they are alive, well, and running a brisk trade; any comment?"

"You see a small part of existence, Ed; what they describe are deformed, twisted residue of nasty post mortem humanity. The real angel, housed as he is in human biology and the roots of things has a huge transforming potential and power. In the deep past this power was occasionally exercised, and seldom with real benefit; I don't use it except on the occasional minute scale. I don't want to be emperor of the world, and if I had I would have long since ceased to exist. Balanced on the edge of power you may last a good part of forever; down on the ground running with it the sandpaper of time would be like razor blades. The rules, the anchoring rules, would be quickly eroded and gone, the angel soon after."

The Fall

"Enough of fallen angels, Josh; what happened the day my friend Dee and Josh Kirkwood went hunting?"

"The root of the matter, the sine quo non of events, is Josh's self confidence and idealistic understanding of himself and mankind; his self definition had no room for weakness, lapses, or failure.'

"Josh got me comfortably settled behind a blind he put up. Before doing this he showed me where he would be -- and it was unquestionably close enough to the quarry that shouts from the old quarry would be clearly heard.'

"I read from a small book of poetry for an hour and a half then walked to the quarry. I carefully climbed down the quarry wall about ten feet, then called desperately to Josh that I had fallen part way down the quarry and needed immediate help; I couldn't hang on very long. I called several times and put the true and earnest desperation in my voice. Josh viewed me as a nasty inconvenience that was rocking the boat and disturbing his life; all he need do is sit quietly where he was and the problem would solve itself. Furthermore I was in trouble because I had gone against what he'd told me to do; it was on my head.'

"After a last desperate cry I leaped head first to the rocks seventy feet below, and I yelled all the way down; then, mid yell, there was a sudden silence. A terrible, tidal wave of remorse washed Josh into paradise and me into Josh; it was Jim looking up at the deck of the Patna from where he'd jumped."

"That curious business of dragging me in to hear from his own mouth the terms of his self definition was probably done to grease his exit?'

"Exactly so."

"The whole thing, Josh, is a little shabby."

"What am I going to say, Ed?"

"It is, and it isn't."

Josh chuckled; "You know me pretty well, Ed.'

"Yes, it is a bit shabby; but after all, I am a fallen angel and have something of a reputation to maintain.'

"But keep in mind something Ed; over the millennia I have borrowed many thulas, but I do not enjoy a perfect success. Had Josh got off his ass and extended a hand the thing would not have happened. I really am strict about my rules. In the Lord's prayer there is a plea, remember? 'Lead us not into temptation.' This is requested of the deity, so such temptations are not exclusive property of 'fallen angels.' I do lead some men into temptation, but it is theirs to yield or stand firm. Josh fell off his pedestal and I have enjoyed nearly ten years of the true heaven; your friendship and the joy of living intimately with Miri, an amazing and wonderful thula. I am in Josh Kirkwood's debt, but stay alert and you will see I pay my debts; I am not talking about being department chairman, though Josh as Josh would not be department chairman in eight years as Dee as Josh has managed. Keep the larger view before you and as an old man judge whether I have paid my debt - and remember, my methods are subtle and usually look like favorable chance."

Then in a different tone and manner; "Ed, I need a favor from you."

"You have only to ask, old friend; if there's any way I can help it is yours."

"When he returns, and remember, it is soon, Josh will pick up exactly where he left, and he will be truly miserable. Please be his friend and offer what comfort you can. Perhaps get him to read Conrad's Lord Jim; remember?!"

Ed nodded appreciatively; "Indeed I will; the ending is searing, not to be forgotten, and makes exactly the right point. Jim faces death a second time and greets the occasion like an old friend, like an opportunity for salvation; he died with 'the look of eagles in his eye.' The real discontinuity is not the fall, but what comes after, what you do with the fall."

"Good, good, Ed; another more practical note. Josh loves bridge and you too would like the game if you studied it a bit. Before they moved here Miri and Josh had a couple with whom they used to play bridge. Miri played partly for pleasure in the game, but more for Josh. After the move Josh was missing bridge. If you and Kim take up the game Miri would happily fall in with it and, though a simple thing, it would be a comfort to Josh. After a year or so you could drop it, or not, as you wish. Also, please stay solid with Miri; for nearly ten years she has been loved, treated, and appreciated for the thula she is. Unlike yourself, she will find the change difficult, and impossible to understand. Little Scott will keep them together, but once he's a young adult they will probably each go their own way. Doubly so in that their bond, while good enough, was never so strong as steel nor hot as fire. Few are, and there is no shame in 'good enough', but there it is."

Thulas II

There was a friendly moment of quiet, then Josh went into the house to get them more beer. When he returned and the beer in hand Ed continued.

"Josh, I want to get to thulas, but I am curious and would like to hear a little more on how you manage to get close to thulas. Is adroit temptation the only door available to you?"

"Not at all; often I court and woo them in the usual manner. The problem has been most acute in earlier eras when they are married, and or when they are in love with another man. Their love must be fairly won; it is an iron clad rule, like the rules of chess. I do <u>not</u> kill or handicap the other man with whom I compete, nor do I subtly bend the thulas."

"Any unusual cases, good stories?"

"Since thulas are found equally in all walks of life most of these would never come to your notice; the swine herder is as likely a source of thulas as a duke. Occasionally I have been enjoying my own thula and another man takes her away; this is not a smart move on his part."

"That sounds more like what I'm after, Josh; any good stories of that type?"

Josh thought a moment; "Didn't you go to Sunday school, Ed?"

"Yes, quite faithfully."

"Remember Bathsheba?"

"Yes; were you Uriah the Hittite?'

"I was, and a most happy hittite at that; Bathsheba was and is a bright memory, though in truth I don't think she compares to Miri, who is something of a thulas thula. At any rate, we were very happy.'

"The David I found was very different from the one you read about in the record. The real David was a charismatic warlord who pretty much took what he wanted and was as much a stranger to remorse as any man I have ever met.'

"What I am about to tell you will seem utterly senseless, even crazy, unless you get a really remarkable man in clear view: the prophet Nathan.'

Josh shook his head in wonder and began to laugh; "Our age has lost sight of the Old Testament prophets circa 1000 BC to 900 BC; these lads were truly men of iron. All over the ancient world everyone kissed the feet of the top men, and obsequiousness was an art form in which, if you were insufficiently artful, you were not only killed but killed in painful and imaginative ways. At the same time in Israel prophets came up to the Big Cheese and said things like 'on a good day, on tip toe, you almost rise to the level of excrement' and proceeded to tell the king 'home truths' nobody, but nobody, would dream of even thinking. Of these supreme tough guys Nathan stood out; not only a man of unbending uprightness but insightful, incisive, with a touch of the poet. Nathan could squeeze remorse and tears from stones. I pinned everything on Nathan being Nathan.

"David saw Bathsheba, liked what he saw, and went after it with his customary directness. I found Bathsheba in tears, badly frightened, and bruised. I was ordered away on campaign and as I left I instructed Bathsheba to wait three to four weeks and then tell David she was pregnant. You know the tale from here: I was called home, conspicuously abstained, and returned to the army quietly sentenced to die. There were no orders to fall back and leave me exposed - exactly how would you manage to leave just one man exposed? No, when I was fully focused on staying alive and killing enemies one of Joab's bully boys put a knife in my back. I saw him coming and stooped a little so as to get a clean heart thrust; it was relatively painless.'

"A reliable friend made sure the incident came to Nathan's attention, and when Nathan finished with David the man was blubbing like a baby; David brought forth big hot tears, but I was the one who dried them.'

"That evening I had Bathsheba brought to my quarters. She stood before me literally shaking in fear. I looked her in the eye and gave her a special wink only the two of us knew -- she fainted dead away. Fortunately I caught her; when she came to she was a very happy thula, and a queen, which she rather liked."

A thoughtful Ed observed; "It was you who wrote the Psalms."

Josh chuckled. "The incumbent could no more write poetry than jump the moon. I wrote a few, but the bulk of them were written by others, and attributed to me. The men around my court were not of a prophetic sternness, and writing a psalm in my name was a fashionable way to curry favor with the king.'

"Your son Solomon is said to have been the wisest man who ever lived; was he in truth remarkable?"

Josh thought awhile; "Your query concerns a man who lived three thousand years ago and, while my memory is organized differently than yours, even so it takes a moment.'

A few moments later; "I'm back in 1000 BC, and ready to go; Solomon was dear to me, but while very quick he was hopelessly self indulgent and divided against himself. He was far from the wisest of men and, as you know, was the ruin of his country. Israel divided under my grandson Rehoboam but Papa Solomon set it up; it would have taken a remarkable man to have preserved Israel after Solomon, and Rehoboam, though an honest and good enough man, was hardly exceptional. It is a curious thing to ponder; how things might have gone had Israel remained together. I'm an angel, and the thing is beyond me."

Ed was weary with ancient Israel and ready to move on; "What was the nastiest thing you ever did to a person harming one of your thulas?"

Josh chuckled; "On more than one occasion I turned the offender into a pig of comparable mass."

"That strikes me as quite an act of power."

"It is; you must reconfigure things from a deep, root level. However the effect is very local and I did it but rarely."

"Why a pig?"

"Typically the Nasty One had harmed others, and I had much company in my sorrow. The fellow sufferers were often destitute and hard pressed; the roast pork was cheering and gave them a leg up.'

"For example, in northern Italy around 270 A.D. I was a blacksmith on the estate of a very nasty senator, a Brutus Cornelii. My thula, Thalia, was a Greek slave of his. Her owner took her against her wishes and hurt her doing so. The owner had another slave who served as his swineherd. This poor man was kept in desperately hard circumstances, and one of his daughters suffered like my Thalia.'

"I transformed the brute into a pig, gave the pig to the swine herder telling him I had seen a magician turn his owner into this pig.'

"Over the next few days the herder came to believe me, and it gave him great pleasure to discuss in front of the pig the upcoming feast, which centrally featured Brutus. He would turn to me saying, 'This succulent little brute will certainly make many happy', whereupon he'd feel the pig's loins and shoulders and verbally divided him up amongst his friends, a shoulder going to Lucius and family, a loin to Marcus, and so on."

Josh chuckled; "You wouldn't think a pig could look concerned or worried, but Brutus lost control of his bladder and shivered in his trotters; Brutus managed the impossible, he <u>did</u> look both worried and concerned. Let me assure you Brutus was no pig philosopher, but he <u>was</u> delicious."

Thula III

William Holding III, chancellor of their university, had fallen on hard times. It turned out his lovely summer home and small yacht had been funded by the university as 'advertising and P.R.'. But there was more; in the course of entertaining several expensive young men who lived in a nearby city, William Holding III had spent additional thousands of university money. Mrs. Holding, friends, and the university board were up in arms. Of course the rest of the world just loved it and, though they were too professional and dignified to admit it, Josh and Ed were members of 'the rest of the world.' With chuckles and shaking heads they made their way through the details, the juicy details. But it was a brief recess from more serious things, and soon Ed brought the meeting to order.

"Josh, I don't know if I'm merely suggestible but over the years I have fallen under Miri's spell; I am become a hopeless thulaphile. Regarding the 'bonzai garden,' I especially love when she is startled or embarrassed -- such understated, exquisite, and delightful expressions! But, as you said, the good things don't come easy, and you must watch closely; I am now a thula connoisseur and share your hobby. How far back does it go?"

Josh chuckles; "I was 'cruising' for thula before the pyramids were a gleam in the pharaoh's eye."

"Was it just you, Ed, or were other fallen angels also attracted?"

"We all were, Ed. Humans are like icebergs; you see the surface and may come to suspect the deeper portions, while for us this is reversed; we start with the underwater portion and go on to discover the surface. From our native perspective thulas are enchanting, shimmering rainbows against a rather ordinary background; it was bees heading for honey.'

"If you are tuned to what happened there are traces of this in the old records. The reason for the traces is simple; thousands of years ago we were not so careful in covering our tracks. As of now you and I are the only ones who know of thulas and the ancient perspective from which they are seen. Modern men review the ancient records with modern mindsets and clean miss obvious things."

Ed was intrigued. "Josh, be specific, give me examples; if possible from sources with which I have familiarity."

"The old Hebrew records speak of 'the sons of God coming down to the daughters of man,' which was referring to us. Thulas are quite rare and there were more of us, so things were a bit crowded; fortunately this proved less a problem than you might think."

"I would guess it posed a colossal problem; in fact, how could it not be a problem?"

"We took over human bodies on the scene and sidelined the incumbent to gardens of pleasant memories, but while we took ownership of human biology it, powerful and pervasive, soon returned the favor and asserted ownership over us. We owned human biology and it owned us - the true marriage that's strong, abiding, and 'til death do us part'. So we angels took flesh in order to be with thulas and soon found ourselves reaching for any willing and ready wench. This sounds pretty randy; but in truth neither more nor less than any other man. 'The sons of God' were noticed since they occasionally exercised unusual powers, powers beyond arranging coincidence, and they all too often made little effort to disguise themselves with the incumbent; thulas and friends recognized someone else was 'there.' But the 'sons of God' coming down to the daughters of man is a small footnote; the Garden of Eden, Tree of Life, and Tree of Knowledge of Good and Evil is much the larger legacy.'

Ed was surprised; "Josh, I see no connection."

"One of the fallen angels, myself, played by strict rules, exactly as I have with Josh. The incumbent is placed in paradise and intermittently chooses between an endlessly intriguing fountain and eating the fruit of the knowledge of good and evil, which, if eaten, would return him to full ownership of his body. For thousands of years I have blunted memory of paradise and the choice; for example, when Josh returns he will have no explicit memory of paradise or choosing, rather there will be intriguing hints, intuitions, a vague déjà vu.

"The original 'Adam' was long before the Jews were the Jews. I sidelined him for fifteen years so I might be with Eve, a typically wonderful thula; I tempted him and he fell.'

"Once returned he spent the rest of his life looking back and pining for 'paradise lost'; never mind that he had acted and chosen in the highest traditions of our species. Never a day passed but he regretted his choice. Adam was an imaginative fellow and he allegorized his story to that of mankind, a fallen and unhappy mankind.'

"In Adam's tale it was he who ate the fruit, and his choice was between the fountain and the tree. Imaginative succeeding seers and poets touched it up in rather predictable ways; symmetry demands there be two trees, not a tree and a fountain, and in an extremely patriarchal society it wasn't long before Eve, not Adam, was eating the fruit. Snakes, ever mysterious, deadly, and malignant were soon inducted into the tale - in fact they were in the story within a hundred years. There really was a fallen angel; myself. The early Hebrews were more historically minded than their neighbors and it is from them we get the tale. To our age it is a myth, but while it has a mythic component it honors and keeps faith with a core of fact; which we are no longer positioned to see."

Josh hesitated; "Our age is an odd one; we see far more and far less than ever before."

Thula IV

"Josh you have answered my questions as promised. There are a thousand other questions I'd like to ask of a man who has been present from the beginning, but they have nothing to do with Josh and Miri Kirkwood. You are on borrowed time and may have other more pressing things to attend. You choose."

"Thanks, Ed; I'd much rather play chess. I probably will never get to play again as your friend Josh Kirkwood. We will see how we feel after the game; perhaps a few questions then."

Ed chuckled; "So we turn to your second passion and hobby," and he started to rise.

But Josh now looked thoughtful, and put up a restraining hand.

"Hold on, Ed. Thulas certainly <u>are</u> a passion and hobby of mine, but they have a significance, a centrality, that goes far beyond enjoying my appreciation. When it comes to thulas I have at the same time told you everything and nothing. It is your call: large scale world anatomy, or chess? As you answer be aware you will almost certainly dismiss what I might tell you as 'metaphysical rubbish'; it will be very out of step with current viewpoints and wisdom. In fact, the only thing to be said for it is it happens to be true."

Of course this was irresistible and Ed resumed his seat.

"You've talked me into it."

Josh thought a moment; "If our universe were an organism, Ed, which tissue and function is mankind?"

"Central nervous system?"

"Perhaps a little, in the sense of feedback, but the primary function is germ cells. Your species is the germ of new universes; you are like DNA. Each of you mirrors and copies the mother organism, and your impression, or copy, is not mush, but rather, since you have language, it is an articulated copy, a copy with details and structure. You carry your copies down to the roots and form special societies that ultimately separate and individuate from the mother organism, or universe."

Josh gave Ed a quizzical look, expecting questions, outrage -- something; but Ed had a preoccupied look and was obviously deeply engaged with digesting what he'd heard. Good!

"The roots are very different from the life we enjoy on the sunny margin, and I use 'society' analogically rather than in literal detail. In the roots you are at an authorial level; you can make fundamental changes, rewrite the rules and boundaries. Remember me turning bad guys into swine?; that is root level reconfiguring. These 'societies' are quite large and ultimately arrive at stability, a statistical feature of large numbers, and develop a culture. We experience their root level cultures as our universe. Like our own cultures on the sunny periphery these root cultures are not planned, but rather evolve. Like peripheral cultures they are stable and objective, even though they have a large subjective component."

Josh smiled; "Dickens' character, Mr. Pickwick, is to our culture what you, Ed, are to theirs, and you are both quite real."

"Damn. Josh, that's quite an earful. You are not, I suppose, pulling my leg?"

"I am not. Remember, Ed, Mr. Pickwick had all his adventures with the lads and Mrs. Bardell and never once suspected he was a cultural artifact. The same goes for middle aged mathematicians in our own society. Both you and Mr. Pickwick are free to devise your own story and account of things. In our time and place gentleman like yourself have evolved a very fine and elaborate story of things that runs in a very different direction. I, for my part, rather like your story, but it is ultimately probably more misleading than helpful.'

"You are too polite to say it, Ed, but at the back of your mind you are wondering what any of this has to do with thulas; the answer briefly put, 'lots.'

"Remember, from a world anatomic angle, I am amphibious, being both of the roots and of the surface. All energy and raw power comes from life on the surface, and all the deep leverage is in the roots; I have both. I have both the power and the leverage to turn a nasty man into a swine; which I have resisted for more than four hundred years. It also means I am uniquely positioned to study root societies and report back to the periphery; also to make helpful adjustments on the periphery.'

"Many, perhaps a majority of these root societies never quite evolve into fully separate universes. Over the millennia I have noticed a pattern: I have never seen a fully successful root society that did not include at least three thulas. Remember; thulas are truly rare, and there are many root societies. Thulas are germ of the germ and I try to see they arrive where it matters. Over the last millennium the number of successful root societies has greatly increased."

A look of dawning comprehension came over Ed's face; "That answers a question that occurred to me earlier but I forgot to ask. I wondered why you didn't take the thulas you have known and loved and after death put them in lovely paradises where you could visit them. The answer is implicit in what just told me: thulas are far too vital to be pulled off course."

Josh smiled. "True, Ed, but in fact everyone is too important to be sidetracked; it would not be right, each person needs to travel his own road without meddling from me. However I <u>do</u> have my memoires, and in the cathedral of my mind I have a lovely stained glass window for each of my friends and thulas. You Ed, a thousand years from now will be visited and treasured: it won't be necessary to win a Nobel prize and write an immortal book or poem. Deeds of immortality are wonderful things, but the detailed flesh and blood man is lost on the usual schedule; but not in your case."

Ed fell to musing and the friends were silent for a few moments.

"Josh, you probably already know this, but your account of our universe and its life cycle has, from my angle, a strong and notable feature; it rationalizes and connects a number of physical constants in our universe that have always seemed entirely disconnected."

Josh smiled. "Of course I am aware, Ed. The truth is terribly obvious and the lads of learning have come at it so ass-backwards they have made a deep puzzle of it. In truth, the universe is the way it is because we are the way we are, while they maintain we are the way we are because the universe is the way it is. The universe being the way it is leaves a number of physical constants arbitrary and unconnected. This is, of course, not very tidy, but their efforts to clean up are an unusually silly whitewash job - in fact, so silly it should have stopped them in their tracks and set them to rethinking the whole business."

Ed wanted complete clarity; "You are referring to the infinite number of universes featuring all the combinations of the physical constants; this gigantic and rather ridiculous assumption in order to have a selection argument of how it is life arose: we are the way we are because if the combination of physical constants had been different we wouldn't be here to ask the question."

Josh stopped him. "I assume you are speaking of the strengths of the four fundamental forces, things like gravity, strong and weak nuclear forces, electromagnetism and such?"

"Yes; had any of these things been other than they are then life would never have happened. For example had the weak nuclear force been .0000001% different, then our universe would be lifeless."

Ed, as usual, was so monumentally quick; Josh was charmed.

"Exactly."

Josh and Ed played their last chess game, which Josh won; Ed had much on his mind and couldn't get properly focused. That evening was the last time he saw his old friend Dee.

Josh and the Tree

Jay's last walk to the tree had been long in preparation, and as this developed momentum there had been a subtle change in his choice; there was now something of the climber and his mountain. Why does a climber climb the mountain? Because it is there. As a kid Josh had read C.S. Lewis <u>The Magician's Nephew</u>. Digory and Polly, with the magic rings and the wood between the worlds, had arrived on Charn, a dead world with an ancient and vast city long since empty and desolate. In the center of the city they found a large rich banqueting hall. In the hall there was a long table at which were seated the rich and powerful people of the now dead Charn. These notables were in a state of perfect preservation, as though only a moment ago time had suddenly stopped. On the table was a note with a bell beside it; the note said, 'ring me, and see what happens. Don't ring me, and spend the rest of your life wondering what would have happened if you had.'

Polly distrusted the bell and note and urged a quick departure. Digory, like Josh and his tree, found the bell irresistible; the bell was duly rung, and no good came of it.

Josh remembered Digory, he remembered Oedipus, he remembered climbers who had suffered and died on their mountains, but eventually, even though he knew in his bones he'd come to regret and sorrow, none of it signified: he had arrived at 'this one thing I do.' The momentum had become irresistible, but it was opposed by an immovable wall: Ann. Ann was very dear to him; dearer by far than all the rest of it combined. He must leave, eat the fruit, but this might mean leaving Ann, which was unthinkable. So he finessed the quandary; he reclassified Ann, and he did this fully aware it was only partly true, but also aware he must see things this way if he was to walk the path that now defined him. He created a fiction, but a vital, crucial fiction.

By now Josh had taken all his close friends to the park, and no one but himself ever saw the tree. In his entire world he was the only one who saw a tree and a choice. The tree was <u>his</u> story, and in a sense his friends were story background. The background component named 'Ann' was very dear to him, but she <u>was</u> background. As Josh walked to the tree he resolutely classified her as background, put her in the background, and held his path firm and close.

Josh plucked the fruit, braced himself for sorrow and regret, and took a bite. The fruit was bitter as he chewed it; nothing happened, then he swallowed.

◼   ◼   ◼

It was exactly like the silver bell, only this time Josh found himself standing in the kitchen of a strange house with a six year old boy tugging on his belt saying, "Come on Daddy, let's play baseball." Then, like a rising tide he realized this was his home and the boy his son Scott. These thoughts had barely surfaced when they were reduced to insignificance; like a wave of briny ice water, terrific remorse and bitter, numbing incredulity hit him like a wall. With Dee's last cry echoing in his ears he despairingly thought, 'How <u>could</u> I not go to his aid!'

Ann and his old world slipped away like dreams upon awakening. Josh never remembered the tree or the choice.

Aftermath

Dee as Josh had all the appropriate memories around Dee's death and these were available to Josh, who, after the initial shock of return, calmed down to a lower grade of remorse. Again he felt a tug on his belt - it was the little pardner. He went outside and played catch with Scott, and in the rhythm of the activity recovered his balance.

An odd and pleasant thing happened to Ed. Two weeks after Josh's return Ed was shaving and getting ready for work when on the television he heard the winning lottery number had been announced several days ago and still no one had come forward to claim the prize. On a sudden impulse, shaving cream still on his face, Ed found his old jacket, the one he had been wearing on his last visit to the Kirkwood home, and wadded up in a corner behind the seam he found the missing lottery ticket. This only deepened the mystery of Josh-Dee; was the 'entity' a fallen angel, or Santa Claus?

Josh-Josh was not Josh-Dee and gradually over time new patterns emerged. Ed faithfully tried to develop a bridge custom, which worked reasonably well for about six months. Josh's bond with his son Scott was stronger and more interested than earlier and soon the two were inseparable pals.

Josh was a vigorous, hard driving man who gave much attention and energy to work. He was a good husband, but was far less attentive to Miri than Josh-Dee had been; Miri sensed this early on and it saddened and troubled her. When Scott left for university his parents' story had cooled to the point they each went their own way. The divorce was amicable.

Miri had three worthy books and a number of good journal articles on her CV, so when a position opened at another university she moved. The new position had a better salary and was congenial; Miri never regretted her move, but she missed Ed and Kim, with whom she had remained close friends.

Over the years Ed and Josh remained cordial, but Ed's status with Josh was always 'one of Miri's friends.'

Ed

Ed was gifted at mathematics and enjoyed a successful career which included chairing the department of mathematics. His two sons proved reasonably trouble free and energetic. Both went into engineering and enjoyed successful careers. In addition, the sons proved prolific and there were six grandkids. Of the grandkids, Hugh, oldest son of Ed's second son, was a greatly loved favorite.

After turning seventy Ed's story with Dee weighed on him and he came to feel strongly it should be saved and treasured, which was an unfortunate wish. If 'successful,' Ed would saddle humanity with yet another noxious religion. The more likely outcome: Humes 'Law' would claim another victim. When someone, never mind how impeccable their record or reputation, reports a thing sufficiently far from agreed on wisdom, then the aberration is attributed to this individual, not conventional wisdom. This is actually not a bad rule; nine out of ten times the aberration is with the individual, but occasionally something slips past.

Grandson Hugh was the hero of the hour and managed to save both humanity and his grandfather's reputation. Ed's zeal to preserve the fallen angels story was more or less coincident with changing his will, which, thanks to Dee, was not a negligible matter; Ed was also getting forgetful and showing a bit of geriatric 'drift'. Ed wrote up his account and in addition had it on his computer. He then confided in Hugh. The alarm Hugh felt was carefully concealed, and the lad listened politely. The new will strongly favored Hugh and these late revelations would only confuse things. When grandpa died Hugh erased the computer and threw out the typed story.

Miri

Miri divorced and moved to her new university appointment circa fifty-four year of age. She was well received in her new situation and a year after arriving she began what was to be by far her most durable and memorable book, <u>Josh</u>. This was a heartfelt, wonderfully observed, and beautifully written account of her ten years with Josh-Dee. Needless to say it irritated the hell out of Josh-Josh, and when journalists and the curious showed up to interview the supernal human being and legend Josh would either hide or tell them to go to hell. Josh, however, was the only person on the planet who did not read and enjoy the book.

The book, as an unintended consequence, brought in its wake a certain celebrity, and at a 'signing' Miri met Roger Matheson.

Roger was almost of Dee grade levels of thoughtful appreciation, and while they never married, he and Miri lived and travelled together for twelve years. There might have been a second wonder book, <u>Roger</u>, in the belly of time, but it was not to be; at age seventy-one Miri had a devastating left middle cerebral artery stroke. This left her in a nursing home, paralyzed on her right side and no longer able to fully understand or speak her native language. Remarkably Miri managed to gracefully sever further connection with Roger; she wished to be remembered as she had been and not devolve into an obligation and burden. Roger gamely tried to visit her but after six months of steady refusal he bowed to her wishes.

It looked as though Miri would end her days as a burden to herself and her nurses, but her last fifteen years were to be the happiest of her life.

John Meadows

John Meadow's life has a storybook quality to it. The first thirty years make dismal reading, and end with John a skid row alcoholic and bum. Then the miracle; he joined AA and managed to control the habit that had ruined him. The second miracle was winning the lottery. The five million dollars was used to develop a head hunting business that was soon fabulously successful. International corporations came to rely exclusively on John Meadows filling their top positions.

One afternoon, John, recently turned forty, was awaiting his flight to London and had nothing to read. He stepped over to an airport bookseller and picked a best seller, Josh. He read it cover to cover on his flight and decided he must meet Miri; easier said than done.

The day John Meadows showed up at the nursing home there must have been a chink in Miri's armor since John Meadows is the only exception on record. Remarkably she enjoyed the visit and seemed to do better with language. John returned to visit every day, weekends included, for the next two weeks. Then John and Miri left the nursing home together, with Miri walking and chatting like a school girl.

When the medical experts got wind of what had happened they doubled checked their scans and records, then contacted the police. It was not possible Miri Kirkwood had walked out chatting the while; whoever walked out was a look alike and foul play was suspected. Miri had a considerable fortune and the motivation for the crime was straightforward. Miri passed every identity verification and convinced Scott she was his mother. She refused their scans and eventually the police and experts scratched their heads and backed off.

She went home with John Meadows, and despite a thirty plus year age discrepancy lived happily together till Miri died painlessly in her sleep at eighty-eight.

Addressing an old woman 'full of sleep and nodding by the fire', Yeats said; 'Many have loved your moments of glad grace, and loved you with a love false or true, but one man loved the pilgrim soul in you and loved the sorrows of your changing face.' Perhaps Yeats caught something of the John Meadows of our world.

Josh

Josh had most definitely made a difference. On his watch the biology department had gone from a sleepy backwater to a sought after graduate program. Josh had clear ideas concerning what needed doing in biology and had his department busy doing it. There was no place for coasting or sinecures.

At fifty-eight he had several important research projects in hand and only a year earlier had published a textbook of general biology that was destined to go through seven editions; <u>Life</u> was the bible of undergraduate biology student for many decades.

Since Miri and he parted there had been several girlfriends but no roots had gone down and the attitude had been a good natured easy come - easy go. His bond with his son was green and strong and Scott was busy and happy in medical school.

This particular Saturday evening Josh had just popped a beer open and was sitting down to watch a world cup soccer match between England and Argentina. Then a stray thought landed; tonight was the welcoming party for the new English Literature professor.

Goddamnit! Josh knew this for silly overreaction but he was perched on a dilemma with very sharp horns. He and Miri had always gone to these functions; it was the right and neighborly thing to do. At last, grumbling and feeling ill used he got his bottom out of the easy chair and started dressing.

Thirty minutes later he was at Professor Donegals home and was sufficiently restored to notice with satisfaction the turnout was pretty good. The new addition was an Ann

Benning, and Josh duly went over to extend the hand of welcome, then, well, get back to the game.

Ann Benning was a trim and attractive fifty-six and as Josh approached her he developed the very odd but irresistible notion that he knew Ann – knew her very well, like he knew himself. As he shook her hand he couldn't help asking, "Professor Benning, you seem familiar; have we met?"

Ann also was puzzled; "I agree; you too seem like an old friend."

They talked a bit, compared universities, trips, and other possible contact points. It seemed they had not met. Ann had many people to meet so Josh stepped to the side, but he did not go home; instead he fell to studying and thinking about Ann Benning. The World Cup, Argentina, and England never crossed his mind. Every now and then he'd come out of his musings only to catch an equally preoccupied Ann studying him! Somehow being around Ann Benning was like a homecoming, like a warm fire on a cold winter evening. He knew things, things like Ann liking the poetry of Walter de LaMare. What nonsense?! But he knew! At last Josh went up to Ann and asked her to meet him for breakfast. She immediately agreed.

Josh hardly slept that night. In the morning he met Ann for breakfast. When they met she said; 'You play soccer, love bridge, and like a bit of apple in your rhubarb pie.'

After breakfast they went for a long walk; in fact, twenty years later they were still walking together. They never figured it out. Ann sometimes wondered if they had been friends and lovers in another life.

<u>Tree</u>

This story has a curious Pedigree. The kernel of the story has been at the back of my mind for many years.

Here it is: At a small mid-western university there is a middle-aged professor of English Literature who is beloved of the Gods; things go his way. All incidents, vacations, lotteries, etc. favor him. A new lady professor intrigues him. The lady professor' husband is a professor of biology, but something of a boor and more a foil to his wife's charm than a flesh and blood human being. The story runs as written till Dee falls to his death in the old quarry. Then, five days later 'Josh' shows up at Ed's house for Dee's usual game with Ed. At the front door Josh smiles at Ed, and asks, "How fares the friend?"

So, I have the idea; twenty five years pass and I decide the time has come to write the story. Then, purely as part of my drill I did something I have found helpful and enriching; in imagination narrate events from the viewpoint of each of the characters. I did this, and to my astonishment the 'boors' view of things opened new vistas; willy nilly he was a fine high minded fellow whose idealism and high mindedness were put to the test and found wanting. The rest of the story was adjusted for this. I have always been deeply moved by Conrad's <u>Lord Jim</u>, and at core the biology professor finds himself a spiritual cousin of Jim, and he too finds himself 'leaping from the Patna'. The story winds up a back door into the garden of Eden, but it certainly didn't start that way!

Story Hour

—◄ ❈ ►—

The whole business looked worn and shabby, and went beyond a few areas of rust on the footrests. The ski lifts at Gunstock, New Hampshire certainly weren't the way he remembered them from younger years. He'd skied out West since then and perhaps this had recalibrated his judgment on such matters. Be as that might, some things hadn't changed; damn he could never forget the charm and beauty of Gunstock. Fifteen hundred feet below and to his left Lake Winnipesaukee looked exactly the same as he remembered, and the spruce, pine, birch, and blueberries were as of yore. How in the year of grace 2080, had Gunstock escaped 'development'? The answer eluded him but he sincerely hoped his kids, if and when they arrived, might stand on Gunstock and ponder the same mystery.

Wes had lingered over his nostalgia and as his glance eventually focused on the path down the mountain he realized he had fallen back a good bit, but his party's quarter mile lead would come to nothing since it was mid-August and their path down the mountains' left shoulder went through lovely blueberries, blueberries of infinite guile which would sidetrack the trek back to the bikes.

Wes' glance down the path brought to mind more than blueberries; not for the first time he put Dr. Dorothy North on the balance and she came up short, at least for his younger brother Matt. Of course it wasn't his business, and he shouldn't meddle, but Matt was such a fine fellow and his only brother; Wes couldn't just stand back and watch the kid make a wrong turn, and to his eyes Dorothy, 'Dot' to friends, if not a 'wrong turn' was hardly a good turn. The whole thing surprised him. Matt was a vigorous and handsome young surgeon of 34 who already enjoyed a large practice and excellent reputation. He could have his pick of women, and until eight months ago he had; and such women! Enters Dorothy, 5' 11" and circa 165 pounds, most of it on her hips and thighs and not enough of it on her bosom, which was conspicuously modest. Her features were pleasant but not greatly advanced from so-so. Wes didn't want a mere showcase wife for Matt, hardly, but he'd like a woman who could be briefly mistaken for a showcase wife before proceeding to reveal she was interesting and had real substance; like Megan. Whereupon Wes both patted himself on the back and blessed his good fortune - what a wife! which brought him to the nub of the matter: Dot was quiet; not as the opposite of loud and aggressive, but as having kinship with rocks and trees. Perhaps Matt found her society shady and restful?

Wes knew he was missing something, a person could not be a professor of philosophy at Harvard and be a total and complete cipher, but the mystery that was Dr. Dorothy North had preserved its virginity despite close and prolonged scrutiny; well, eight months of scrutiny.

Thus musing his way down the mountain Wes at length found his party ambushed and trapped in a patch of blueberries. Just before leaving for the outing, with thoughts of blueberry pie in the evening, Wes had put two quart size plastic containers in his pack. With the air of a conjuror pulling rabbits from his hat, Wes produced these containers and directed the parties energies towards them; there was 110% acceptance of the blueberry pie project.

A pleasant half hour later they were once more on the path for home and Wes, yet again musing and strolling, fell behind. This time Matt's musings had practical issue, rather drastic issue: this evening, after the blueberry pie he would call a story hour. There are few more certain and reliable means of separating quick and interesting from slow and dull than having the one to be measured tell a story. Firmly, and with a commendable sorrow, Wes resolved to put the dunce hat on Dorothy, and settle it so conspicuously on her head that even the besotted kid brother must see it.

This well-intended 'surgical' maneuver had another motive, a less selfless and heroic motive. Wes was a Harvard professor, a professor of modern history (1840-2000). In the course of pursuing his duties he made a close study of the movies of olden times. Recently he had come under the spell of <u>Terminator</u> and itched to share the story. Yet again he fell to musing on the story!

Here it is: Malignant machines nearly destroy humanity, but in the eleventh hour a charismatic leader, John Conners, rallies humanity. Soon it is the machines who quiver on the edge of extinction. The wily machines, as clever as they are malignant, develop a time machine to send the ultimate killing machine (which looks exactly like a man) back to the late 20th century to kill John Connors' mother Sarah; no mother, no charismatic leader. Humanity comes across the time machine immediately after the terminator leaves to kill Sarah Connor. The machine is still active and John Connors sends a young man back in time to protect his mother; the man he sends is his father. It's the old, old story where the steps taken to avert a dark destiny are the specific means of bringing it about.

Sarah is a young woman making her way in L.A. as a waitress. She is soon engulfed in a terrifying wave of deadly events that make no sense. A young stranger appears to help and protect her, and his attitude towards her is one of reverence; she's the mother of John Conners, his greatly respected leader and savior of the race. He tells Sarah she is a legend - and then she <u>knows</u> he's crazy! But events are so strange that finally, while hiding in a culvert under a road, she turns to the young man and in a hungry and intense manner asks him to tell her about her son. Wes got goose bumps thinking about it, and he vowed to share the goose bumps. Mulling over his upcoming story Wes nearly ran into Dorothy and Matt, who had slowed to a stroll so as to savor the golden late August afternoon.

Matt was pleased at his brothers arrival; "Wes, your timing is perfect; what are your thoughts on Harvard's new course on Nigerian art?"

Wes had no idea how Dot saw such things and didn't want to give offense, but…hell, probably best to label crap for what it is.

"That course and the impulse behind it is misguided nonsense. Ping pong, gin rummy, basket weaving, and a host of cousin activities all deserve cultivation and appreciation, but not at Harvard. One must draw the line, and occasionally it requires the nicest judgment, but Nigerian art probably comes in behind gin rummy as a candidate."

Matt chuckled; "You sure?"

"Absolutely, no possible confusion; and in our day there would be general consensus on this point."

"How is it the course is on offer?", asked the curious younger brother.

"One of high and mighty ones owes a favor, is infatuated with an enthusiastic and beguiling young professor, or has such a professor as an in-law; something of that sort. We all need to just take a deep breath and remind ourselves 'this too shall pass'."

Matt was curious; "Wes, you said 'in our day there would be general consensus on this point'; this suggests another time might divide on the question. Has there ever been a time when Harvard offered basket weaving equivalents?"

"Indeed; 1960-1980, and not only Harvard but all our best universities. It was an unusually silly spectacle. The underlying culprit was the liberal truism that all cultures quo cultures are equal; you were not allowed to even think one culture might be richer and possess greater resources than another."

Matt looked a little skeptical; "Wes, I want to be clear on this; you say Harvard professors a hundred years ago looked at our symphony, with its many complex and varied instruments that evolved over hundreds of years, our scale and nomenclature, our rich literature for all instruments and combination of instruments, then looked at stone age tom toms and whistles and couldn't conceive that on matters musical our culture might be a little richer?! You <u>are</u> pulling my leg, right?"

Wes looked at his brother's face and had to laugh - at moments like this he'd kill for a camera.

"No, Matt; I'm sharing the true word."

Matt struggled with his incredulity; "Then surely the moment must have been precarious; like the fat emperor pirouetting naked before the crowd - someone is going to chuckle and suggest his fat ass is bare."

"No; our academics were all gifted trapeze artists who, like gods, strolled the thin wire of incredulity for more than twenty years: straight faces, no chuckles, profound solemnity."

"OK, I'll bite; who broke the spell, the enchantment?"

Wes thought a moment; "Life is seldom so black and white, so simple, but perhaps as much as anyone the moral philosopher Alasdair MacIntyre is your man."

Professor North, as is the way with rocks and trees, had hitherto remained silent; she now found her voice and thoughtfully creaked into motion.

"That's how I understand it as well; perhaps his book After Virtue would be the specific event."

Wes was both very surprised and greatly charmed; "So Matt, not only a man, but a book!"

Then turning to Dot; "Dot, what are your thoughts concerning Nigerian art at Harvard?"

"Everything you've said is true, but I wouldn't be much of a Harvard academic if I didn't put in a few qualifications. Imagine you are invited out to an expensive restaurant for a good meal. After dinner a hostess comes around with a tray which has several varieties of both cakes and cookies. You look them over and pick the most enticing. Suppose instead the hostess asks which you liked best, cakes or cookies. Not very helpful question, is it? In place of this or that specific cake or cookie we are offered abstract classes, classes divorced from particular circumstances such as being quite full and having had cake last night; one small tasty cookie is what is needed - preferably a cookie with nuts and chocolate."

She continued; "When you offer Nigerian or Western cultures as abstractions, I am in the same quandary. Getting down to cases: if the cultural dessert tray included a renaissance painting with a number of cherubs, a Bela Bartok quartet, and a curious smooth stone from Nigeria, I'd have the stone off the tray in a jiffy."

Wes was curious and leaped to the heart of the matter; "Do you think 'culture' is a useful word and idea?"

Dot was charmed at his quickness; "I'm not sure, but probably not; it might be better to approximate 'culture' with three or four clearer and simpler ideas, one of which would be 'custom'. But that's neither here nor there; things are as they are and we are muddling along well enough."

Wes was interested; "I'm not sure I follow your thought; can you make it clearer?"

"Sure. The root problem is 'culture' is so general and inclusive as to have little specific clear meaning. For example music and customs are separate distinct strands of 'culture' but these strands are very different. Our music is much richer and more varied than theirs and it is silly to pretend otherwise. However, social customs, things like our shaking hands while they bow to each other, really are entirely relative and there is no question of which is richer or better. Now for the unfortunate foolishness: customs are relative therefore cultures are relative therefore music is relative. The root problem is the unfortunate word 'culture' and its tendency to such pernicious syllogisms."

By now they were back to the bikes. On the way home they stopped at the general store in the village of Gilford, where, to their surprise, they found four rib eye steaks. Charcoal, lighter fluid, beer, and potatoes were scouted up and they once again headed home.

Soon after getting back to their cottage the weather turned cold and it began to rain. While Matt and Wes worked on getting the steaks grilled, Megan, an acknowledged expert on pie matters, worked on the blueberry pie while Dot 'nuked' the potatoes and made a salad.

The temperature continued to fall and the fury of the storm increased so Megan decided to cozy the common room with a fire and gave the assignment to Wes, who was delighted since the weather and fire helped shape events toward story hour.

Everyone had a stake in the meal and all were hungry from an afternoon of hiking and biking, but beyond this the meal was superb and appreciated and enjoyed as a thing apart.

After the meal Wes and Matt lay down on the rug by the fire while the women picked up the kitchen. When the kitchen had been restored Megan and Dorothy joined them with port and liqueurs.

As they savored their drinks Wes unveiled his plan; "Tonight I want to honor an ancient custom of our species; let's tell stories around the fire. We will each tell a tale, and may the tales be shining and memorable. I will start, then Matt, followed by Dot, and ending, as a special treat, with Megan."

Matt chuckled; "Megan and I know what this means, but Dot this is all new for you; Wes has yet again come across an old movie he liked. Story hour with Wes is always good, so I'm in - girls?"

The 'girls' were nothing loathe and soon they were deep into the adventure of Sarah Connor with the Terminator. Wes took a few creative liberties with what he viewed as the bare bones of the story and in consequence improved and enriched what was already a strong story.

Matt followed with <u>The Monkeys Paw</u>, an unusual story of a treacherous talisman with the power to grant wishes, only the wishes are brought about in such a way as to bring ruin and misery. For example, you wish for a million dollars. The next day your wife is killed in a car accident and it turns out she had a million dollar life insurance of which you are the beneficiary. Matt had a deft way with a story and the effect, while unquestionably dark, was powerful.

They were now arrived at Dot's turn, and Wes had misgivings; the girl seemed harmless enough and his measures struck him as excessive and severe - ah well, too late for regrets. Dorothy, if she was on the banana peel, didn't seem aware; the brazen hussy was actually smiling! Wait! Was that a twinkle in her eye?! Wes was rocked; he'd never imagined Dot could do a twinkle, and a rather beguiling one at that!

Dot turned to Wes; "Wes, you choose: the high challenging path or the low easy path?"

What game was this? Wes, minding his digestion and feeling contrary, ventured; "Low and easy."

More twinkling, "I'm sorry Wes, I didn't phrase that correctly. Let's try again and remember, you are a son of Harvard and could never let the crimson down. Choose again; low and easy, or loitering in the swamp?"

Wes considered; "Are there mosquitoes?"

"Clouds of them and they're hungry."

Wes shrugged his shoulders, "Let's do low and easy."

"Good! Then tonight's the night! We be three Harvard professors and a gifted surgeon - if we aren't up to task, then who is?! Let's do it!"

Wes spoke for the rest; "What is our task, the one for which we might even suffice?!"

"We are going to do some comedia d'l arte. This is an old Italian art form where the players, or actors, are given a situation and then improvise the play on the wing. The whole play is off the cuff. I've always wanted to do comedia d'l arte and never have until now. Guys, get into your roles like they are your skin; let's be worthy successors of those gifted old players!"

The 'guys' began catching her excitement, began anticipating, and Dot didn't let things coast; she got right down to it.

"Here's the scene; we are going to move our fire back to 990 A.D. in a small rural inn in northern Germany about 40 miles south of the Danevirke. The time of year is late fall and there is a dusting of snow on the ground. It is after supper and present around the fire is the landlord, which is you Wes, a wise and good natured priest, which is you Megan, and a wealthy merchant-trader, which will be you Matt. Also present is a forty something soldier whose business is not stated, this is me!"

"The background is as follows: In 960 the Viking King Harold Bluetooth was baptized, with the consequence that Denmark is partially Christianized. In the early seventies the Vikings crossed the Danevirke and raided Holstein. In 974, by way of retaliation, the German Emperor Otto III assaulted the Danevirke and Hedeby (an important Viking fort and trading center). The whole area came under German control and the Germans established a strongly garrisoned fortress. This caused dismay and anger amongst the Vikings and weakened Harold's prestige. Harold's son, Svein Forkbeard, an unrepentant heathen, began asserting himself even though his father was still nominally king. Svein spearheaded the recovery of the lost Danevirke area and by 983 the German fortress was carried by a ruse and burned. Eventually Svein seized power and Harold died of wounds in 986. By 990 the Germans are all gone; Svein Forkbeard remains heathen, but tolerates Christianity; Svein is looking to England, and the German frontier is quiet."

"Enjoy a little general sociability around the fire and after visiting a while bring the conversation around to the stupid folly of the various heathen religions. After working the topic a bit you need to ask my views."

"Matt, as a trader you have been as far east as India and have seen several of the thousand faces of Hinduism."

Turning to the rest of them; "Get into your parts; let's create something wonderful."

After she paused she turned to Matt; "You're on."

Merchant – turning to the Landlord, "Winter seems to be falling early and heavy. Right glad I am to be by this warm fire with pleasant company."

Landlord - "To be sure the fire and company are pleasant, but the fall has been easy, and even now is no more than seasonable. I think you got your yardstick in some gentler clime. Where do you call home?"

Merchant - "My home is in northern Italy, but I don't think I've been there more than three months at a stretch these last eight years. My grandfather was German, but long ago followed opportunity south and we've been there since. Now it seems I've grown too soft to face a German winter."

Priest - "Yes, and there's some things you'd just as soon not get used to."

Landlord – addressing the priest, "It seems you know my mother-in-law; a German winter is a playful kitten by comparison." Turning to the merchant, "What brings you so far north, friend? All the money is down south - up here it's only misery and death."

Merchant - "So I hear, but also it is reported that these evils are leavened with furs. The wealthy beauties of the south think nothing of my sufferings and much of furs. Perhaps it is possible to extract the furs and leave misery and death undisturbed."

Landlord – laughing with genuine mirth, "A most excellent plan! This plan is a cousin to one my father devised for my education when I was six."

Merchant - "Don't leave us hanging, tell of this plan."

Landlord - "To extract the black stripes from a wasp's belly and leave the sting." The landlord's mirth became general, with the merchant leading the laugh against himself.

Priest – speaking to the merchant, "But surely, my son, even in Italy the tales of the savage Northmen must circulate. Be assured they are no idle jest. Truly, I believe their obdurate hearts are beginning to be thawed by the gospel, but spring is by no means in sight. In their northern fastness there yet lurks a most savage heathenism."

Merchant - "Good father, you mean well by me, but I am quite inured to heathenism. My travels have taken me as far as India. I have many times seen the utmost savagery and the quaintest tomfoolery's. I defy your Northmen to get me out of countenance."

Landlord - "Well, Sir Iron Face, permit me to offer up a specimen of our northern fare. Several years ago my nephew Cuthwulf was traveling north of Birka and spent an evening in a peasant home. What do you suppose was the object of domestic reverence?"

Merchant - "In a general way I would imagine it was some image cast in stone or wood, or possibly a grove of trees."

Landlord - "The sun would be up tomorrow were I to leave you, alone and unaided, to arrive at the privy member of a horse."

Merchant - "And so it would be! That is a surpassing strange bit of heathenism."

Priest - "It is but another instance of the self-evident general truth that the myriad forms of heathenism are alike in their idle foolishness and impotence."

The Merchant and Landlord raise their mugs and say; "Hear, hear!" Then, for the first time, they all noticed the pointed silence of the soldier.

The landlord turns to him; "Come my friend, surely you can raise a glass to the discomfiture of the heathen!?"

The soldier responded with; "I will do both more and less - I'll drink to the true faith, may God ever preserve it; as to the folly and impotence of the heathen, I venture no guess."

The landlord, being of a waggish turn, said, "Good Sir, pardon my presumption, for at first glance I wist not ye were a philosopher."

The soldier smiled pleasantly; "My good host, your first glance was shrewd, for I am no philosopher. All I claim is a working pair of eyes - I've seen what I've seen."

The landlord said; "I trust you aren't referring to inward, spiritual eyes?"

The soldier, sipping his beer, said; "No, the eyes in question are the ones I see you by - a task hardly requiring spiritual discernment."

The landlord turned to the others; "Tell us your tale and let us judge for ourselves what it portends for the heathen."

The soldier, putting his mug to one side, answered; "Fair enough." He paused gathering their attention fully to himself, then proceeded; "It is now very quiet up around the Danevirke, but, as you all know, a few years back it was a hornet's nest of activity, and a man literally took his life in his hands to be up there. As God willed it, I was a young soldier of nineteen when, in 974, our Emperor seized the whole area of the Danevirke and Hedeby. I was above the Danevirke off and on for the next ten years until Svein Forkbeard finally threw us out and bolted the door. During these ten years I came to understand, respect, and intermittently hate the Norse. They have many Gods. Of these I mention Thor and Odin. Thor warms the heart and it is impossible not to like him. Odin freezes the heart. The more one tries to understand him, the more incalculable he seems - and the more one fears him. The man who does not distrust and fear Odin would have to be in the grip of a strange madness. Odin is the All Father, but it is mostly kings, magicians, poets, and Earls who traffic with him - the common man gives him a wide berth. There are as many sides to Odin as there are grains of sand on the sea shore, and the best you can hope of most of these sides is a deep game of cat and mouse, where Odin is the cat, you are the mouse, and the rules are beyond your ken. These are his good sides. His bad side is dark indeed and can be sensed in a desperate and stricken field, and in scenes of pitiless slaughter and utter ruin. His animals are the wolf and the raven. The dark side is clearly demarcated and is associated with war; in this mood he is frequently called by an older name, Ygg. I bear Odin no love, and I introduce him only because he is the central figure in my story. At any rate, in 978 I was in a party of eighty men raiding high above the Danevirke. Our captain was both a good soldier and a good man and I want to pause to drink a toast to Captain Athelston, may he rest gently in God's hand."

All solemnly raised their glasses and echoed; "May he rest gently."

The soldier then continued; "By a considerable bit we were the farthest North we'd ever been and, since our pillaging had been only modestly successful, the general feeling was we should be heading back. So mid-afternoon on a late fall day very like the one just passed, Captain Athelston called a halt and was in the act of ordering a return to camp. Then - curse his sharp senses! - Gurt interrupted and pointed to a distant flock of ravens circling some trees and cawing. It was nearly a mile distant and we could not clearly see what had raised the hubbub. Most of the men were for leaving the ravens to their party and getting on home. A minority were for investigating, and since these included the captain, we headed towards the ravens."

"The day was cold, gray, and a light snow had begun to fall. I don't care for ravens on a sunny day, and on this bleak day I couldn't have felt less like joining a party of ravens - the situation felt bad to me from the very first. I chided myself for an old woman and hurried to keep up. We arrived soon enough, and about one week after a Blot, or pagan sacrificial festival. Hanging from the trees were the bloated and blackening corpses of men, horses, chickens, pigs, cows, and dogs. Not far from the grove was a small long house and at its door an old man and a young man appeared. Upon seeing us they grabbed axes and spears and ran towards our party. Our archers brought down the young man long before he could use either ax or spear, and the old man was soon overpowered and tied to a tree. Some of the soldiers pillaged the house and barn and then set them afire. While this was going on I talked with the old man and discovered the grove was sacred to Odin and he and his sons were priests of Odin. Our group reassembled by the grove, now stronger by two cows, one horse, several weapons, and a bit of jewelry. By now it was late afternoon, with a gray sky and snow bringing evening on ahead of schedule. The reasonable thing was to stay where we were and leave in the morning, yet the place was so forbidding it was our unspoken agreement to leave and camp elsewhere."

"In the midst of getting organized for departure I had a sudden sense that something had gone terribly wrong. My mind raced to place the wrongness, and from the look on other men's faces other minds were similarly employed. The lurid yellow of the burning buildings was unchanged. The rotting corpses were the same, the late afternoon seemed the same, the - it was the silence! The ravens had all along been quarreling and cawing amongst themselves, now, suddenly they were as quiet as the corpses. I was just realizing this when every eye turned to the top of the nearby meadowed hill. A lone man, about three hundred yards distant, had appeared, and was almost certainly the missing son. He surveyed the scene below, then raised his ax and gave a terrible hoarse cry that at three hundred yards was preternaturally strong. He began running towards us with an impossible swiftness."

"I sensed the approach of a thing of unspeakable menace, a dark destiny. Some of our archers were sufficiently cool to get off several arrows, but this seemed like throwing straw at a bonfire, somehow it didn't signify."

"By now the whole situation was becoming unreal and like a nightmare. There seemed to be an immense slowness and futility to our every motion. With painful slowness, as though in honey, I turned my back on the scene, and with year long by year long steps began to leave. It seemed as though I were being sucked back, and the more desperate my efforts the greater the pull. Finally I gave up on fearful desperation and filled my mind with an old chant. I don't know whether I sang aloud or only in my mind, but in the event the sucking tide began to ebb. At a distance of two hundred yards, and on the other side of the field, I felt things return to normal."

"I now risked a backward glance and beheld a scene of terrible slaughter. A single figure moved on the field, and it turned towards the trees where the Norse were tied. As the figure approached the trees it gradually walked more slowly, then there was a cry of heart piercing anguish and desperation; "Oh, Father, flee!"

"The pitiless figure slowed even more, but kept advancing, then suddenly there was a great cry, and the advancing figure was torn to pieces before my very eyes. Somehow the young Norseman had deflected the killing rage onto himself and thus spared his father. With Odin there is never a question that anything but blood will answer - if not that blood, then this."

"The entire disaster had taken very little time and it was now just before twilight. I waited until my teeth were talking amongst themselves and I was shivering with the cold, then I returned to the grove. My party had been torn to pieces and were often not recognizable; there were no living men except myself and the old priest, the wounded Viking having died."

"Eventually I cut the old man down and gave him a warm cloak. Neither of us said much, and I only asked him would he be all right. He seemed numb, but motioned for me to leave, which, after a bit I did."

"That is my story; of a party of eighty that entered Odin's grove I alone left. What does it portend for the heathen? Judge for yourselves, but as you judge remember Samson, and ask yourself why it was that he always went alone amongst the Philistines."

There was a prolonged silence, eventually the priest said; "You tell a most fell tale. Before judging I would be interested in how you understand your own tale. For example, was the young Viking a berserker?"

Dorothy, stepping out of character for a moment, looked around; and asked; "Shall we take the fire back to 2080? Megan replied earnestly; "No, leave the fire where it is, and in character answer my question."

Dorothy shrugged; "So be it. Certainly the young priest may have been a hound of Odin, or berserker, but this would relate to what happened only as a house cat is related to a lion. In one way what happened is easily seen, in another it is quite opaque. The various parts of my story worked to summon Odin: The gray day, the rotting corpses, the burning buildings, the ravens, our fear, the burning rage and faith of the young priest, these things called to him and he answered."

The priest nodded; "The point about Samson being that when Samson slew one thousand Philistines with the jaw bone of an ass he would not have spared any Jews in the area - he was horribly dangerous to all men, and the Jews knew it. This suggests that like Odin, Jehovah has a dark side; will you own this suggestion?"

The soldier answered: "I must, and I do."

The priest settled back and said; "Thank you. My judgment is that I join you in not judging."

The landlord said; "I will not judge", and the merchant answered, "Nor do I."

A silence followed, and all eyes turned to Dorothy, who ripened the moment till it was full to bursting, then; "Let the fire return to 2080."

Gradually, like a returning tide, their cozy family room in Gilford New Hampshire re-established itself and present reality. Yet the silence lingered; finally Megan spoke.

"Wow! For me story hour is finished; <u>anything</u> else is anticlimactic. God Herself couldn't follow that story. I want to sip my port, wind down, and think. In about ten minutes perhaps some Scrabble, or Wes' new romantic comedy, which has received very favorable reviews."

These thoughts were shared by all, excepting Matt, who seemed preoccupied. They sipped their port and liqueur in a companionable silence, while Matt quietly excused himself to find his computer and look something up.

Five minutes later the spell had faded, and Matt was back, looking extremely pleased with himself. The new romantic comedy was chosen over Scrabble, and in the event delighted one and all; some things are so straightforward not even critics, despite their cleverness, are able to trip or confuse themselves.

After the movie, still chuckling, the friends drifted off to their several rooms. When Dorothy and Matt had closed the door to their room Matthew gave Dot a hug and a kiss; "Sweetheart, your story was wonderful, brilliant. The comedia d'l arte dream, long deferred, is now fully realized. How many years before <u>Quizzical Sketches</u> did you hold the dream?

"Many years before the Sketches; I picked up the idea my second year of univ....", Dot trailed off into silence.

Matt and Dot stood face to face studying each other attentively; finally Matt said; "You've known who I was right from the beginning, haven't you? You have played and hunted the hunter from the get-go; and the result - now you're cornered!"

Matt dropped to both knees before her and held her around the hips; "I'm not letting you go until you agree to be my wife: and remember, I'm an Olympic hugger; I have hugged for America."

Dorothy gave him an affectionate kiss; "I accept, accept with all my heart. Matt, I planned on telling you when we got home; it was to have been quite clever."

Matt laughed; "Wes and his story hours! Well, this one flushed you out of hiding!"

※　※　※

Wes was by habit an early bird, but the next morning he was quietly putting on his boots even earlier than usual. He was on vacation and nobody else was stirring, so why the early hour?

Yesterday afternoon as they were returning from Gunstock he had asked Matt to take an early morning walk with him. The walk was to get them away from the cottage for a man to man talk about women in general and Dot in particular. Now, after story hour, he found he didn't have much to say; Dot's story was many things, but as a maneuver to expose wallflowers it was a thermonuclear grade fizzle. Wes, with speed and silence shot out the door neck and neck with the dawn.

As he walked along another thought intruded itself; after the story he and Megan had discussed the Viking era and commedia d'l arte with Dot, and what with her flushed and rosy cheeks, animation, and wonderful transforming smiles, why she looked ten years younger and could easily be mistaken for a showcase wife - and a young one at that. Hell, he was pretty sure he had seen a dimple, and he loved dimples. No indeed, he had no advice for the kid brother;

besides, you really, really shouldn't meddle. He'd been taken in with Professor North's Harvard persona.

Lost in these thoughts he almost ran into Matt, who was headed back towards the cottage.

Wes quickly slipped into outrage mode; "What about our early morning walk?! I thought you had been kidnapped?"

"I'm sorry, Wes; too happy and full of thoughts to sleep, so rather than disturbing Dot I took myself off for a walk. It was too early to bother you. But this is perfect; come, walk me back to the cottage and I'll tell you a great story."

This was entirely agreeable and Wes allowed himself to be mollified.

After pulling off a graceful 180; "Well, brother, let's have the story."

"Do you remember - what was it, three years back? - you insisted I read <u>Quizzical Sketches</u> by Thalia Pointe? What a delightful and clever book! I was utterly charmed and for the first time in my life I decided I must meet the author, who, I don't remember how I got the impression, was a younger woman. Well, 'Thalia Pointe' was a nom de plume and despite multiple efforts, some of them rather ingenious, I got nowhere. The proverbial blank wall."

"Three or four months later, via the friend of a friend of a friend I bumped into Dot on an internet chat room. We conversed many months on the internet before agreeing to meet. I was charmed by her conversation, and then her person."

Wes could only take so much and he interrupted his besotted brother; "Matt, Dot's person is OK, but aren't you pitching it a bit high? Charming? Matt laughed; "Wes, you're a clever fellow and a good brother, but never, at any point in your life, have you understood the finer points of bottoms; Dot is bottomed like a goddess - 'one shade the less, one ray the more had half impaired that nameless grace'. Stick to things you understand and let me get on with the story."

Matt paused, then; "So, for many months I've been caught in a quandary: I'm captured and beguiled by Dot, but I'm haunted by Thalia Pointe and am unable to make any final settlements until I meet her. Fortunately the life of a surgeon doesn't lend itself to soliloquizing in poems or mooning around, because otherwise I'm afraid I might be doing both."

"Fortunately a savior appeared and cleared the way."

"Who might that be?"; Wes was genuinely curious.

"My older brother, of course."

"Me?!"

"You! Last night you led us on another of your story hours. When Dot seized the chance to realize her dream of doing comedia d'l arte, her excitement jogged my memory, which I double checked after story hour. On page 81 of Quizzical Sketches she mentions her as yet unfulfilled dream of performing comedia d'l arte. Thalia Pointe and Dot North are one and the same!"

"Well, what are you waiting for?"; asked Wes.

"We're not; last night I proposed and was accepted. We plan on getting married either today or tomorrow; you're to be best man. There is a nice little chapel in Laconia that is ideal for such things."

"Hold on! Don't you think this is rushing things? Perhaps let the ink of your resolve dry just a little?" Matt laughed, "I'm in too good a mood, too elevated; I'm kidding. Of course there is family and a bit of ceremony. No date is set. Relaxeth a bit, brother."

They were nearing the cottage as Matt had an idea; "Wes, you should make a story of our story, or perhaps a movie."

"Too late for that; it has already been done; and done well, almost a hundred years ago."

"Really?"

"Yep, another of those old movies; ever hear of <u>You've Got Mail?</u>"

Matt went into the cottage to start breakfast while Wes walked a bit further. The gist of his thought was that story hour was kind of a reverse of Matt's Monkey's Paw story: Yesterday his deepest wish was to leave Dot behind, while today she was joining his family and he couldn't be happier.

Story Hour

The provenance of this story is rather prosaic - I lifted it, with modifications, from my first novel, <u>And the Morning and the Evening Were the First Day</u>.

This novel was mostly written between 1989 and 1995 and not published till 2000. I like it very much, but no one else shares my enthusiasm. Of the few hardy souls who made it cover to cover all they seem to remember five years later is the brief short story. This is an effort to free the 'captive'.

Shantria, or The Great City of Hope

—◄ ▓ ►—

The alarm went off, and for a moment Ben was disoriented; then he remembered. Yes, it was Saturday morning, and 7 o'clock to boot, but Monday morning at 8 he had an important chemistry exam for which he was not remotely prepared. Hence the rigors of a 7 A.M. alarm on a Saturday morning.

Ben sighed, toyed with shutting off the alarm and going back to sleep, then, with resignation dragged himself out of bed and into the morning. As he brushed his teeth, he became aware of a bird singing outside his window; there was something very peculiar and different about this bird song. In one way it was much as usual, but it also seemed to come from another place and time, a place and time of which he had only the vaguest recollection. The recollection was so vague it was hardly there at all, and soon the bird sounded much as any other bird; however, there had been an odd moment, and it lingered at the back of his mind.

Ben navigated many tempting diversions on the way to the library, but 8:45 A.M. found him beavering away in a secluded corner of this citadel of scholarship. By 11:45 he was a spent force and voted himself an early lunch.

The lunch greatly refreshed and strengthened Ben, but not for further study; the thought of returning to the library possessed no charm. Rather than bucking a strong current, and it <u>was</u> Saturday, Ben decided on wiling away some time on his guitar, which of late he had neglected. Ben had a locker at the music building and directed his steps this way. He spent a good half hour working on a new song compounded equally of charm and guile. At last, reasonably satisfied with the new song, Ben was musing with a guitar in his hands. He absentmindedly improvised his way through a series of chords and fragments of melody. There was a gentle momentum, enough so that when he came to a sudden stop it caught his attention. What?! Why had he stopped? Then it came to him; that last cord was not only strange and rather dissonant, but it was out of step with everything he had been doing for the past five minutes. It was not only that the strange chord didn't fit or join, but rather it was an important part of some other music, significant music. It was like that teasing bird song, only more so.

What does one do with such odd moments? Clearly there was nothing to be done, but it dropped the curtain on his musical moment. Ben returned the guitar to the locker and headed once again to the library. He was settling into his corner when he sensed motion and looked up in time to catch a passing coed, and receive an almost electric shock of disorientation; the girl was familiar, but she belonged to a radically different context. It was almost as though a leopard, properly found in zoos and jungles, were treading the library. Almost immediately the jolt was gone, and in pale confusion he exchanged glances with a young woman he had noticed in his chemistry class. The coed was tall, blonde, and shapely. Upon observing the pale shock and confusion of her fellow chemist her face broke into a smile that was like blue skies and sunshine appearing between dense banks of ominous clouds.

"Ben, isn't it? When I got out of bed this morning I knew I should take the time to apply at least a bit of makeup. But no, I put chemistry first and hurried to the library. Now, poor innocent victim, I almost shocked you out of your chair! My sincerest apologies. Good luck Monday".

With Ben stammering incoherently the coed chuckled and went about her business. In truth, whether in or out of makeup, the coed was a treat to contemplate and Ben felt the perfect fool. What was it with this particular Saturday?! Eventually he more or less recovered his equilibrium and, after a fashion, 'studied' an hour before giving it up as a lost cause. Instead he went for a good hard bike ride. After a shower he made himself a sandwich and considered the upcoming Saturday evening.

He should spend the evening with his chemistry book, but he'd had no luck in that direction and deferred such efforts till Sunday. Saturday evening with the lads was always pleasant, and the football game this evening looked good. There were two problems with this choice. Firstly he would invariably drink too much and he didn't want a headache tomorrow morning. Secondly, and more subtly, he sensed something important was hanging over him and choices made now seemed a little more consequential than usual. If the smart choice was to open the door to novelty and the unexpected then he should attend the English department's bash, which was scheduled for 7 p.m. this evening. This was a yearly gesture at bridging the chasm between the liberal arts and the hard sciences. It was proper that such 'hands across the campus' efforts be made, and it was proper, or so felt the science students, that it be avoided. Ben partook strongly of these very sentiments, but if new possibilities were to be courted this was clearly the arena. Just before 8 p.m. Ben, in a skeptical frame of mind, headed for the English and history quadrangle. He planned on giving Novelty no more than two hours to find him, then off to join the lads.

There was a moderate amount of traffic around the quad. People were dressed casually and the atmosphere pleasant and low key. Nice. The central common area was attractive, spacious, and interesting. The overall layout was a large rectangle with carpet, modern décor, and modern art along the walls. Off center there was a twenty by thirty foot room with wood floor, fireplace, and old stuffed leather furniture. This inner sanctum communicated with the containing larger area by two large doors.

Ben strolled the area and then headed to get a drink. The choices were champagne, red wine, white wine, and various cheeses. Ben was disgusted, but not surprised. If God had meant us to nibble and sip on Saturday night he would have, well, he probably wouldn't have bothered with us at all. On the other hand, if there ever was a schedule more suited to deliver a chap headache free to his books Sunday morning, Ben couldn't think of it. So, armed with white wine and cheese more benign in appearance than its mates, Ben resumed his stroll. There didn't seem to be any goddesses on the premises but there were a number of reasonably attractive girls. Ben, feigning an interest in the wine or modern art on the walls attempted to engage them in conversation. These efforts were received with polite disinterest; whatever it was these girls sought clearly did not include him. Ah, well. Ben strolled on, brain idling in neutral.

Suddenly he came to sharp focus; what had captured his interest? Something across the room. He studied the opposite side thoughtfully, trying to place what had attracted his notice. Then he had it; it was a modern painting! Ben was intrigued; few people took less notice of modern art than his mother's son. Furthermore, it almost goes without saying the picture didn't fit or belong; like everything else today it's home was somewhere other than this liberal arts building. Ben crossed the room and stood before this dignified alien prisoner. The painting was abstract and impressionistic with no specific context or content, but it strongly suggested the spires of a beautiful city viewed at sunset. Up close he realized it could mean many things to different viewers, and he wondered at the clear impression it had evoked. For once he effortlessly passed a Rorscharch test!

Musing on the strange city of many spires he drifted into the cozy inner room. There, in a corner near the fire, he noticed a cluster of fellow science majors patiently serving their time. He recognized the tall blonde from the library, and, most surprisingly there was Mohan Rao! Mohan was a physics major and a guiding spirit amongst the lads; he should, beer in hand, be presiding over the football game. In truth Mohan as a sports commentator and critic was far ahead of the T.V. personalities, and infinitely more amusing.

For a moment Ben forgot manners and just stared.

"Mohan, are you lost? Did a liberal arts strike team kidnap you?!"

"Kind of, but it's a bit more complicated than that. And you, Ben, you're not at the football game either."

"No, I'm not; but, unlike you, I won't be missed."

In response, Mohan wagged an extended pinkie, ostentatiously sipped his wine, and simpered, "The sport buffs will just have to struggle on without me."

When the chuckles died away the tall blond from the library said, "We seem to form a little group; let's introduce ourselves. I'm Jan Cooper and my major is chemistry. Gwen, you're next."

Gwen was a quiet, very attractive mulatto; "Pleased to meet you. I'm Gwen Brown and my major is English literature. Jan and I are friends from high school."

To Gwen's left was a short, slightly overweight, shy looking young man afflicted with pink cheeks. "I'm Sam Rost and my major is mathematics."

Mohan was next; "I'm Mohan Rao, majoring in physics. Home is Cincinnati."

Ben was the last; "I'm Ben Linde. I'm pre-med and haven't settled on a major, but most likely chem or biology. Furthermore, I have a plan for our little group."

This last sentence surprised Ben more than the others. The strange 'captive' painting had lit some deep fire that just now pushed to the surface.

"With the honorable exception of Gwen we are strangers in a strange land. I want to do something memorable, something to confuse and intrigue our cheese nibbling, wine sipping, literary colleagues."

"Do you plan to moon them?" asked a curious Mohan.

"Possibly, but not just yet. For now I'd settle for a literary experiment, something to baffle and amaze them in their very own backyard. If that doesn't do the trick, then, as a parting bow we can treat them to a collective moon."

Sam interrupted, and surprised everyone; "Ben's right, Mohan. If we lead with the moon it will shock and distress Gwen, and none of us want that. Tell us about the experiment."

"Partners, I'm feeling my way and suggestions are welcome and encouraged. At this point I see us as lonely and beleaguered science types doing a bit of brain storming. I imagine we are a group of good friends on a quest, and we will take turns with the narrative of events."

"What do we seek?" prompted Jan.

Ben was clear on that; "A city. But this city is very different from wherever it is we begin the quest. The city is more advanced, more beautiful, better in all matters of importance. However, it is very, very inaccessible; though much sought it is but seldom, if ever, found. Our quest is not trivial, not for a moment."

A thoughtful silence fell on them. Then Gwen spoke; "Our homes should be in a small rural community featuring a simple culture and simple techniques. The year is divided into very clear patterns and rhythms."

Gwen paused, then; "We live by primitive farming and herding. Our home is in a forest, which we have cleared enough so we may farm. The herding is at least as important as the farming, and our community seeks pasture in nearby foothills, foothills to impressively rugged mountains."

Sam of the pink cheeks interrupted; "Gwen, everything you describe feels right. The quest is the curious thing; it exacts a regular tithe on the best and brightest of our land. Many leave to seek the city and they either turn back soon after leaving the foothills, or they never return, and so pass from memory. Year after year after year the city remains shrouded in mystery."

"This greatly simplifies things", said Mohan; "I don't like the odds. I'm heading out to plow the fields, find a wife, feel the sun on my back."

Jan put her oar in; "That's what we all do, Mohan, but the city is at the back of our mind and beckons to us as a candle flame beckons to a moth."

Ben liked this; "Jan's hit the thing on the head. This urge to quest pulls at some more than others and eventually, from our generation, we are the ones who must go. Now, how do we organize and plan our quest?"

There was a quiet moment then Gwen spoke; "I think you are the leader, Ben. You have our confidence and you never act without consulting us. The mountain portion of the quest would be on foot with backpacks. Getting to the mountains we use pack animals. We will need to carry with us the means of survival; things like bow and arrow, fishing line, perhaps medicinal herbs."

Sam was curious; "What pack animal? Horses? Llamas?"

Gwen was thoughtful; "No, I don't think we have horses or llamas. I sense our animal, but he's not there yet. This is odd; I also sense a name, but it too eludes me. I'll get back to you."

Mohan picked up the development; "A cousin of mine comes with us to the mountains and then returns with the animals. Now comes a peculiar twist. We are not casual, we mean business, and this reveals itself in two ways. First, in view of no return traffic from the city, we elect to avoid the obvious and easier route through the mountains in favor of a harder and less used trail, a trail that is more of a goat path. The idea being the sensible route must have hidden perils."

"The second point is a real humdinger; we make a binding commitment to the quest and each other. No one, singly or collectively, returns home except through the city; our home is made a hostage of the quest. This is not quite 'victory or death', but it is very strong. Are we agreed?"

There was silence, then Jan spoke; "It is a strong commitment, but it feels right."

The others all nodded in agreement.

Ben started to speak, but was interrupted by Gwen; "I have helped set up the quest but I'm not going on the quest. This quest is a science and mathematics endeavor. Every story needs an audience and I will be the founding member of an audience, which hopefully will enlarge."

Then Gwen smiled; "If your literary efforts should limp I want no part of the farewell moon."

"You sure, Gwen?", asked Mohan. "It's odd, but it seems to me you are part of the quest. Besides, God forbid, if things should limp the final gesture would be much stronger and more effective with your participation."

"Thanks, Mohan, I think", laughed Gwen; "I'm sure; yours will be the glory, or the ignominy. If worst comes to worst, Jan will be there to anchor the final gesture and give it class. So, let's get started; who's first?"

There was a pause, then Mohan began; "With your blessing, Ben, I think I narrate the first leg of the quest."

Mohan looked around, gathering them with his eye, then, when in possession of their close and undivided attention, he began.

"Had we left in early spring the low country would have been more passable but the mountain passes would still be snowed in. Translated to our calendar we left in late April, or early May. The first day on the road the weather was picture perfect and questing and picnicking seemed variations on but a single theme. The second day out the rain came, and stayed with us for a solid week. The country was low and boggy and it seemed we never were free of mud and swamp. I would like to report that we were spared bugs, but it would be a lie; we were plagued by clouds of stinging and biting insects. It was quite, quite miserable. One week into the quest we at last met the mighty Ghinja River and began following it north into higher country.

Two days later we came to the Opengey Bridge, a relic of an earlier imperial era. Though nearly a thousand years old it was still standing, still took our breath away, and still was technically far beyond us."

Mohan sipped his wine, and was about to begin but Sam interrupted; "But we didn't cross the Opengey Bridge, did we, Mohan?"

This startled Mohan; "No, Sam, you are quite right. Since we planned to travel by goat path we continued on another three days to the Salsana Bridge. The Salsana bridged a much narrower gap than the Opengey, but the gap was a rocky gorge and the river a boiling madness. Who, or how they ever got that bridge across the river was truly mysterious. The Salsana was high, and beautiful in the way the art on these walls is beautiful."

Mohan hesitated a moment, "They, the Salsana and our modern art, share a certain spare elegance of line that is 180° from the baroque, or our friend Rubens."

Ben wondered a little at how Mohan was going on over the Salsana, but then, out of the corner of his eye, he noticed they had attracted a few onlookers. Good.

"Unfortunately the perfection of the Salsana was marred by a fifty foot gap in the very middle of the bridge. A rough but serviceable cable had been placed across this gap, and depended from the cable was a simple seat on a runner. There was a second smaller cable beside the larger cable and this allowed a person to pull himself to the opposite side. The arrangement was simple and effective. We arrived at the Salsana towards evening and made camp on our side of the Ghinja. In the morning my cousin Primus and the pack animals would return home, while the rest of us would shoulder our packs, cross the Salsana and begin our journey."

Mohan paused a moment; "Gwen, any luck on the pack animals?"

"Not yet, but it will come."

"Well, I'll give you a hint; unless I'm much mistaken the hind legs are a little longer than the forelegs."

Mohan returned to his narrative; "That was a wonderful evening. We had a roaring fire and a regular feast. Primus came into focus as never before and stood in for hearth and home; we had no certainty of ever seeing either Primus or home again. In the morning, with our packs and equipment rearranged, we bid farewell to Primus and crossed the Salsana, then…"

Mohan came to a confused halt and sat quietly, lost in thought. The silence stretched and stretched. Finally, when Ben was about to interrupt to get things back in motion Mohan once again looked around and gathered them with his eye.

"That's not what happened. This curious quest of ours seems to have a life and will of its own. The water and power of my tale seem to run in channels laid down before I opened my mouth. Before I share what happened allow me to suggest guidelines for your tales; respect the story, and if you should sense momentum or direction follow this sense rather than getting inventive and creative. Why? Why do I say this? Because I have a hunch. I've had a very curious day with many odd moments and I came to this party tonight thinking that I should, that something would happen. I think I came for this story."

Mohan paused, then "Here's what happened. All of you crossed uneventfully and I was the last one. As I crossed, the supporting cable snapped and I fell. This particular fall was certain death; the eighty foot fall would give you a thumping but not much more, but the rocks and water would finish you several times over. I had time to fully register my situation, but instead of slamming into rocks and current, I fell into a patch of pale, golden mist; that's the last thing I remember. I never hit the water. But I must have hit the water! Perhaps I had an out-of-body experience and parted from my body before impact. I don't know."

They were all quiet, then, with a twinkle in his eye Mohan continued. "I'm finished, but before I hand over the tale I want to once again warn against being too creative. Don't tell how you miraculously tumbled so as to miss death many times over, and each time by millimeters. Downriver you cleverly braved and escaped pirates, liberal democrats, cannibals, and government bureaucrats. Bypassing every obstacle, you rejoin the quest just in time to save it from utter disaster. I repeat, do none of these things. Rather than lead the tale try to follow it."

"So, I was the first victim; from failing hand I pass the torch..."

"To me', picked up Sam Rost, "with numb horror we saw you fall. You <u>never</u> hit the water. We all saw that patch of golden mist; it came between you and the fast approaching river and you never came out the other end. Beyond rhyme or reason you were just gone. We spent the rest of the day looking for your body and must have gone four or five miles downriver before returning to the Salsana Bridge. That night was as bleak and melancholy as the night before had been merry. The next morning, with first light we broke our fast and prepared to travel, but we hadn't gone a hundred yards when Jan, looking back to the bridge, stopped us all."

Jan interrupted, and she looked both startled and confused; "It was the cable and chair on the bridge wasn't it Sam? They were exactly as they had been when we first arrived the morning we crossed".

"Exactly so, Jan. It was spooky; most unsettling. It was as though Mohan had never fallen. Ben, upon seeing the cable and chair, pointed us to our trail and suggested we walk while we pondered. The day was beautiful and the scenery enchanting; the sting of strangeness soon ebbed. In truth pondering the cable and chair got you nowhere. The mind just slid away from the thing and could get no purchase. Soon every last one of us gave it up, without comment. There was nothing to say, and we said nothing.'

Sam paused, and let out a sigh; "The next five days were very beautiful, and coupled with the rhythm and fatigue of walking we were healed of our loss and the associated strangeness. The quest knit us together and gave significance, meaning, and healing. We were calm, and in a way even happy. Mohan was very dear to us, and our closing ranks so smoothly and quickly seems odd, but only in retrospect. We were bound tightly to the quest and each other. There was no turning back, and our turn was probably just ahead; no one blinked or schemed to escape or duck. When it came, it came. And then we put it from our minds."

Mohan smiled and interrupted; "Is it possible I detect a trace of guilt, O Mathematical One? If so I hereby absolve you."

Sam thought a moment; "No, not really, Mohan; I'm thinking aloud, trying to understand."

"Mid afternoon on the sixth day since leaving the Salsana Bridge I was walking about thirty paces behind Ben. The trail was 4 feet wide at its widest places and 8 to 10 inches at narrow points. On our right there was a sheer drop of about 500 feet and on our left it was a near vertical stone wall. As Mohan said, it was more a goat path than a real trail. This trail needed steady nerves. Ben and I were in the lead and we had passed a narrow spot about seventy yards back. Jan would be coming to it as we were rounding a corner. Then there was a cry of surprise and alarm. I spun around and, … I'm not sure what I saw, but it was electrifying. Quicker than quick I took off my pack and raced back, all my attention on who I went to help, none on the trail. It proved the wrong focus; I hadn't gone 30 feet before I placed my foot wrong, tripped, and went over the edge to begin a 500 foot trip to rocks. My state of mind was peculiar. Most of my frantic attention was still on, … on you Gwen! You <u>were</u> there! Jan never fell; it was you! Your ledge had given way and you were left hanging desperately by your fingernails."

"He's right', said Jan; "You <u>were</u> there, Gwen, just ahead of me. Somehow you managed to shrug off your pack and you were hanging by your arms to one small rock. The interval between your rock and either end of the trail was too far for any sort of swinging or climbing. You needed a rope, quickly, or you were finished."

"Whoa!', interrupted Mohan; "Sam, please don't take this as a criticism, merely an observation on the narrative art; it is generally frowned on to veer off in new directions and leave the protagonist 500 feet above rocks and unsupported. Did you just hang there studying Gwen's dilemma?"

Sam looked puzzled, and after a moment Ben spoke; "Mohan, it is strange to tell but I'm not sure Sam saw what happened; he fell facing towards Gwen and never looked down. I'm afraid I will have to tell his story. His journey to the rocks was never completed. As with yourself he fell into a golden mist and never emerged."

Sam was thoughtful; "Ben's probably right, Mohan. My last thoughts were of Gwen. I never noticed any golden mist, or, for that matter, rocks. Sorry, friends, but my turn at the narrative helm has been very brief."

Gwen, who had remained silent, now spoke; "A minor reality check; we are telling stories, we are creators, and things are exactly as we say, neither more nor less. I specifically stayed out of this story, hence I'm not in it."

Jan answered her, "Gwen, you are both right and wrong. Mohan was the first to sense this, but something strange is happening. Yes, it is a story, but it is not 'just' a story. We can sort it later. Right now we need to go with the current, let it happen."

Jan paused, then continued, "At the risk of derailing our project I want to make this clear. Your part in our little experiment, Gwen, will be to pick up the narrative from the rock where you are hanging. But first, I will take Ben aside and tell him my version. Then, with Ben as independent witness we will compare the two narratives. Remember what Mohan said; respect any sense of momentum or direction."

Jan took Ben out of the room and then after one or two minutes they returned. Both looked serious.

"O.K. Gwen; pick up your story."

"This may work better, or worse, than you imagine, Jan. While you were gone with Ben I have been as neutral and quiet as I can manage hoping to sense a direction. The direction I sensed makes my story very brief and very odd."

"I held that rock utterly resolved to still be there when a rope arrived. But my hold was minute, fingertips and not much else, and the pain and strain were terrific. I was becoming frantic. Then, in the rock itself, at about chest level a golden mist developed. This is hard to explain, but it was as though the rock became transparent, then misty, then golden. Somehow the mist was comforting, and second by second my attention shifted from my screaming arms and fingers towards the mist. I don't even remember letting go, it was merely a small part of the dawning importance of the mist. Finally, I shifted into the rock wall and lost awareness."

There was a stunned silence. Ben and Jan stared at each other in mute wonder.

"That's right, Gwen; you fell <u>into</u> the rock wall. From where I watched, your final motion was entirely into the wall, no component down the wall."

Ben interrupted; "Gwen, Jan described the changes in the rock wall exactly as you did. But let's not think of this now; let's go with the current. Jan?"

"First I want to complete Sam's story. Now that Gwen is aboard, if briefly, Sam's situation is much clearer. At the beginning Sam had very little questing urge, but he did have a deep, deep love for Gwen. Gwen was different, she was a guiding spirit amongst us and the motor that got us off our bottoms and on the questing trail. Sam came on the quest because leaving Gwen was inconceivable. However, once on the quest he proved a very strong addition due to a steadiness and practical turn. His narrative is entirely in keeping with this; he fell with his eyes on Gwen, not the rocks beneath him."

Jan paused, and there was a twinkle in her eye and a puckish smile on her lips; "To my ear Mohan and Sam have affected a bard-like dignity and grandeur. They think they are Tolkien, or something. I'm just folks, and going forward the story will be humbler and in a lower key."

"In summary; mid-afternoon on the sixth day since leaving the river a strong and hopeful expedition of five people was down to two members. I am proud to say that neither myself nor Ben thought of turning back; we would either make the city or join our friends. No middle ground."

Ben and I sorted through Sam's pack for whatever might prove useful, and planned our next move. The original plan to avoid the main trail had only given these golden willowisps more opportunity to prey on us. We both agreed to get back on the main trail. We also agreed it was high time that in all things we needed to become cautious old women. It seemed to us the willowisps worked the margins; ordinary perils became more perilous. By this I mean strong cables broke, and rocky paths gave way around these things. If we managed to get through the mountains we might actually make it."

"I still think this assessment more or less correct, and I did manage to survive into early fall."

Sam interrupted; "What happened in the fall?"

"In the fall there was only Ben; but I'll get to it soon enough. The intervening months were interesting, wonderful, and hard. Over the next two days we managed to join the main highway and then the wonders began."

"Remember those incredible bridges back at the river? Our path now was on the travel routes of a long gone and very advanced ancient civilization. We were like stone age people amongst the ruins of New York City. The roads, bridges, tunnels, and mighty dams took our breath away. Eventually we arrived on a vast plateau that stretched for hundreds of miles and had an average elevation of 8 to 9 thousand feet."

"Over the summer we crossed this plateau and passed through two immense ancient cities and one smaller city. There were clusters of people at our own stage of development and these people lived mostly by herding and hunting. They proved friendly and we traded with them. Also, there was the occasional trading caravan crossing the plateau. For the most part we lived by hunting. Ben was quite good, and the water supply favored us."

"How so?", asked Gwen.

"Water was scarce, and if you staked out a water hole something was bound to come along."

"However, care was needed since the willowisps also used the water holes."

"Damn!", interrupted Mohan; "How does a willowisp stake out a water hole?"

"Ben never agreed with me on this. He felt strongly held ideas were drafting every patch of sunshine into their scheme. Here's my story, and again, Ben never bought into it."

"One late afternoon Ben was crouched behind a bush eighty feet from a water hole. I was perched on a nearby rocky elevation enjoying the setting sun. I happened to look down and to my eye there was too much sunshine behind and to the right of the crouching Ben. The light everywhere was fading, but not here; if anything it was brighter. I was frightened and looked around; thirty feet behind Ben was a crouching predator creeping up on him."

"What sort of predator?", asked Sam.

"Like one of our mountain lions, only a little larger and the hair a little longer."

"I leaped up, grabbed a large stone, and started shouting. Ben turned just in time to see my lucky throw strike the cat. The animal was startled and bolted. The previously bright patch of sunlight was gone, just another dim patch of shadow."

"I told Ben my story, then I reminded him of our observation of many months earlier; dangerous margins become more dangerous and were manipulated by the willowisps. This cat had been taking the evening air and been put to work by the wisp."

"Ben laughed and assured me the cat was only being a cat, and at sundown the light would play tricks. Life and death come into sharp focus at a water hole."

"Ben and I had been friends since childhood but that summer we became more, and had events been different we would have made a home together. We were very happy."

"In the evening, around the fire, we discussed the golden wisps and how to understand them."

"No one had seen or heard of our golden wisps. No one had seen so much as a trace of the great city. Several of the traders had traveled far beyond the mountains. Our quest became more and more mysterious. Were the wisps recruiting for the city? Removing nuisances and trouble? Was the city a story created by the wisps to attract pilgrims, which might be a rare delicacy for a spiritual predator? Just as dragons greatly favor the flesh of young princesses perhaps wisps treasured pilgrims."

"In the complete absence of any tangible evidence for the great city I gradually came to favor the city as a wisp story to attract dinner. Indeed, so much so that but for Ben I would have wintered with the herders and returned home in the early summer."

"How did Ben see it?", queried Mohan.

"This is going to surprise you guys, but the story Ben had carefully concealed philosophical depths. Ben was struck, and stayed struck, by Gwen's disappearance into the very substance of a stone wall. To him this could only mean our world was an elaborate metaphor of some sort, that things were very different than we thought them. Practically speaking ordinary thinking and conclusions regarding the quest were almost certainly missing the point. Ben was as clear as could be on this; if ordinary conclusions were not reliable or trustworthy then all we really had was the quest and the promises to our friends. Ben never wavered. But, much to his credit, he enjoyed my speculations, which he thought very clever, and was good natured about the whole business. However, every morning we matter-of-factly continued our journey to the eastern margin of the plateau."

"It was vital that we either be tucked in with the herders or out of the mountains before snowfall. We were on track for this, but without much margin. We decided to walk an extra hour each day; we did this by striking camp every morning at first light."

"In late summer we were nearing the eastern margin of the plateau. We crossed a vast ancient city that was on the shore of a large lake. This was breath taking. The ancient builders replaced wisps as the focus of our thought. Ben didn't much miss the wisps, and in truth, neither did I."

"The lake drained on its eastern flank in a series of spectacular waterfalls. Not even the builders could keep our attention; mother nature was center stage. I especially remember the rainbows against the deep blue of the early autumn sky."

"By mid-autumn we were within a week of being out of the mountains. One beautiful autumn morning we were just emerging from a coll into a lovely valley. The coll itself had been very narrow with sheer rock walls on either side. The passage was still rocky, and, while widening, was not yet open. The coll was heavily shaded by the sheer walls but as it opened up into the valley the sun was quite dazzling. I am going on about this since upon emerging from the coll I walked right into a golden wisp and out of the story. The END; and it's embarrassing. Nothing dramatic like the rest of you guys. Pleasant stroll, inattentive, gone; that's my requiem. Ben, you're up."

"Wrong, Jan. Inattentive yes, but incredibly lucky; you were within two to three seconds of an unusually miserable death. I was behind you and saw what happened. In the last idle moments do you remember any insects?"

Jan thought a moment, then; "Ben, there were always a few insects; where do you think we were, a vacation poster?"

"There was a cloud of huge wasps, almost the size of humming birds, that came out of the coll just behind you. They were going for you like there was no tomorrow. You stepped into the wisp only just ahead of them. I didn't even have time to yell, let alone do anything useful."

"What a jolt! One moment your friend and love is strolling along ahead of you, then you are alone. Jan's absence really hit home; I missed her terribly."

"Before picking up the quest I want to make a small correction. Jan was 110% correct about the waterfalls on the eastern edge of the plateau; they were stupendous. However, they were not the sole work of mother nature. The ancient builders had devised a descending series of dams and lakes and connected them by water conduits that turned turbines. The dams, over several thousand years, had leaked and broken in various ways. The resulting pattern of waterfalls was sublime."

"But back to it; the next few days were a kind of a midnight of the soul. I was a travelling automaton, a man getting through the day by pure habit and will. Then, in the early afternoon of the sixth day since leaving the plateau this ended."

"You too strolled into a wispy patch of sunshine?", asked Sam.

"No, I crested the last mountain summit and there it was; Wow, whoopee, hot diggity damn was it something!!"

"The wisp to end all wisps? Another waterfall, or ruined city? What did you see, you extravagant bastard!"; Mohan had little time for rhapsodies.

"The city, the city, THE CITY!" That first moment was utterly searing; never to be forgotten!"

"Just beyond my mountain it was as though our world ended in a vast, incomprehensively vast, shimmering wall that stretched to and beyond the horizon in every direction; left, right, up, and, impossibly, down! Our world ended, and you could as easily see forever down as forever up. The walls were like a living, coruscating rainbow of color. Beyond, we, we…"

Ben was faltering; then he stopped. "This is hard to explain, but beyond the rainbow wall you could see shifting scenes of the city. For example, there might be a palace garden and courtyard scene with lovely walks amongst trees and fountains. There were men and women of great dignity and loveliness. As you looked you had a sense of seeing a piece of a much larger thing; the walks connected widely with other things, and the other pieces were all there too, and they subtly deepened and informed what you could actually see. The world of the scene was there! looming and immense behind the scene. And these scenes seemed to be clear and near, then vague and far. The shifting scenes were many, varied, and stretched in all directions to the horizon. Many of the scenes were both terrible and fascinating. I saw a lion of immense size and savagery hunt down and tear a man to pieces. And always the world of the scene stood behind the scene and made it more real and vivid than I can describe. I looked, and looked; I don't know how long I stood studying the scenes. At length I turned to descend the mountain and enter the city."

"I never explicitly put it out on the table of my mind, but I assumed this stage of the quest would be a stroll into the kingdom. Wrong!"

"In what follows I never met another traveler or even animal. I never stopped to wonder that traders passed this way and never saw anything but another mile of their

journey. I saw only the city; and how it <u>did</u> beckon and call
to me!'

"At length I came on to the level and walked, and walked,
and walked, but never seemed even an inch nearer the city.
I walked through the night, and in the morning it was as
though I had not taken a step. Late in the afternoon of the
second day it seemed as though I might have gained just a
little on the city. I stopped neither for food nor water, but in
truth I felt no thirst or hunger. The third day was different;
it was as though I were hiking up a steep hill. Soon this
changed to a sense of walking up a vast sand hill. Finally it
was a hill of the proverbial molasses in January. Each step
was a thing of infinite weariness and effort. I had long since
passed through all my physical reserves and margins. Then,
when further efforts seemed impossible and utterly futile,
but you knew you would <u>never, never</u> stop, some barrier was
crossed and I approached the city with hugely increasing
speed. I was not running, but rather is was as though the
earth itself was a racing current. By now the speed was
terrific, vertiginous, and the current rose in the sky to travel
nearly vertically in an asymptotic approach to the vertical
wall, I was racing to meet infinity, and the view gradually
become misty, and golden; but this was not a patch of golden
mist, this was a golden dawn that stretched to the horizon
in all directions. That's the last thing I remember."

Ben fell silent and the members of the quest were left
numb and empty, just looking at each other.

Mohan broke the silence; "It cannot end here! We've
come too far, endured too much. This will never, never do..."

While Mohan groped for words Gwen interrupted, and
this interruption was like the very hand of fate; "I remember
the name of our pack animal!"

Then, at exactly the same moment, they all said, with a guttural starting deep in the chest, "hrom!"

As they said this they looked at each other as though for the first time, and they remembered, and understood.

Finally Mohan spoke; "Sometime it is important that it be said clearly what we all know. Friends, to your feet; huddle up."

They got to their feet and stood in a close circle. There were many curious onlookers. Mohan spoke quietly and for them alone; "On the other side of the great divide we spoke of the golden wisp. On this side of the divide it's emblem is the stork. There is only one way into the city; you must be born in!"

"Friends', and Mohan spoke with fierce triumph, "Our quest did not fail; we are in the great city!"

They parted quietly and walked away slowly, viewing all things in beauty and from a great height. Except Ben.

Ben had barely cleared the inner sanctum when an earnest young lad noteworthy both for his art and his liberalism pulled him aside.

"That was a very intense game. What is it?"

This brought Ben completely back to his scene in the many and varied scenes of the great city. He thought quickly. This was too perfect.

"The game we just played is called Shantria. It is all the rage at Oxford. There is a friend of mine studying English lit at Harvard and I learned it from him. The idea is very simple; you plan a quest with five or six other people and then take turns with the narrative. That's all we did."

Shantria was 'all the rage' for several months. None of the original members ever played again, despite eloquent coaxing.

Gwen was haunted by the picture of Sam falling to his 'death' with his eyes and attention fixed firmly on her. Socially speaking Gwen was in the stratosphere and Sam was in the basement. Her interest and attention were received as manna from heaven. After university they went on to build a home together and were and are very happy.

Shantria

This story is my own favorite and has the oddest background. The germ of the story arrived while reading Jack McDevitt's The Eternity Road. The background to McDevitt's novel is about 800 years after the apocalypse, which happens around 2100; our world pretty much ends. Humanity survives into a new primitive dark age. An intrepid band of predominately young adventurers who live somewhere near Kansas or Missouri decide to walk to the east coast to see what they might see and recover old books, such as Mark Twain and Churchill, of whom they have a few tantalizing fragments. Such expeditions have been launched in the past - and never returned. As they make their way east they encounter hi tech artifacts they don't understand and they start dying by barely comprehensible accidents.

The tale was gripping, and in the very middle of the story I had my epiphany. But first some necessary background.

Rightly or wrongly I see our natural history as being larger and more complicated than is commonly apprehended. The life cycle of the butterfly includes caterpillar, cocoon, and butterfly. As I see it our life cycle also has three stages, and we typically take the first stage for the whole story. Those of a religious persuasion see two stages: our immediate present stage, and the post mortem pie-in-the-sky stage. We are the caterpillars, with butterflies in the hereafter. In my scheme there are two stages post mortem, but NOW is the butterfly time; with all its shortcomings 'these are the good old days'. So I always find myself with a wicked urge to turn the conventional scheme around 180°.

Now for the epiphany. McDevitt has his hardy band dying off one by one as they make their way to a deeply mysterious, perilous, awesome east coast. I have my band 'dying' off one by one on a journey to a wonderful city, but 'dying' is really being born into our world i.e. we are in the wonderful city.

So, I had my idea, and I liked it very much, but there was no 'launch', no pen to paper. Then, three to four weeks later, I got launched by music I was composing. I liked my musical creation but couldn't quite get an ending that felt right - and I tried many different endings. Finally I had 'it', and it was quite simple, a chord repeated three times. But, and this is hard to explain, while the chord was exactly 'right', it simultaneously didn't fit, was profoundly out of place. I was launched - when Ben got out of bed that Saturday morning he kept bumping into that 'chord'. By the way, it is now many years downstream and that chord is still exactly right and doesn't fit at all. But by now the story and the song are very linked, each evokes the other.

These stories are at right angles to things usual and familiar. What would happen if Rainbows suddenly disappeared? How might the fallen angel tell the story of Adam and Eve? A walk in beautiful mountain country as a thing piercing and bleak beyond measure. A young terrorist dreams the impossible dream, and a young Harvard professor finds his weekend strangely frustrated and what comes of it. The reader will return from these and other stories to find his own world richer, stranger, and more beautiful.

TRUE DIRECTIONS

An affiliate of Tarcher Books

OUR MISSION

Tarcher's mission has always been to publish books
that contain great ideas. Why? Because:

GREAT LIVES BEGIN WITH GREAT IDEAS

At Tarcher, we recognize that many talented authors, speakers,
educators, and thought-leaders share this mission and deserve
to be published – many more than Tarcher can reasonably
publish ourselves. True Directions is ideal for authors
and books that increase awareness, raise consciousness,
and inspire others to live their ideals and passions.

Like Tarcher, True Directions books are
designed to do three things:

inspire, inform, and motivate.

Thus, True Directions is an ideal way for these important voices
to bring their messages of hope, healing, and help to the world.

Every book published by True Directions– whether it is non-
fiction, memoir, novel, poetry or children's book – continues
Tarcher's mission to publish works that bring positive
change in the world. We invite you to join our mission.

For more information, see the True Directions website:

www.iUniverse.com/TrueDirections/SignUp

Be a part of Tarcher's community to bring positive change
in this world! See exclusive author videos, discover
new and exciting books, learn about upcoming events,
connect with author blogs and websites, and more!
www.tarcherbooks.com